THE GIRL WHO LOVED HISTORICAL ROMANCE

A BOOK OF
FIRST CHAPTERS

TESSA DARE
COURTNEY MILAN
JENNIFER HAYMORE
TIFFANY CLARE
SARA LINDSEY
MAGGIE ROBINSON*
*WITH BONUS ALTER EGO

Table of Contents

The Girl(s) who Loved Historical Romance..ii
Schedule of Releases iv

Tessa Dare...1
   One Dance with a Duke 2
   still available 20

Courtney Milan.. 21
   Trial by Desire 22
   Unveiled..34
   still available 40

Jennifer Haymore 41
   A Touch of Scandal..42
   A Season of Seduction 50
   still available 58

Tiffany Clare 59
   The Surrender of a Lady 60

Sara Lindsey.. 74
   Promise me Tonight 75
   Tempting the Marquess 86

Maggie Robinson/Margaret Rowe... 97
   Mistress by Mistake 98
   Mistress by Midnight 104
   Mistress by Marriage 114
   Tempting Eden 118
   Any Wicked Thing... 123

The Girl(s) who Loved Historical Romance

The six authors[1] who have contributed to this volume have a great deal in common. We all write historical romance. Our debut novels will all published in the short span between March of 2009 and October of 2010.

But we have more in common than that: We knew each other before any of us sold a book. That sounds like an incredible coincidence. After all, not a lot of people sell books. How likely is it that six people who know each other would sell historical romances in close succession?

It's actually not that surprising, though, if you understand how we met. We met online, and we bonded over our common love for reading and writing historical romance. We sent each other excited e-mails about the latest books by Eloisa James, Julia Quinn, and Joanna Bourne. We met at conferences, to exchange thoughts. When we started writing our own books, we sent each other drafts and asked for comments.

And when we started sending our work out for publication, we commiserated about rejections together, and squealed for each other when the good news came. We asked each other questions about the business of writing, too: What to do with copy edits, what to expect from agents, who to use to build a website.

We made the transition from readers to authors. And so it's particularly fitting that we present our work to you the same way that we started: together.

While we all write historical romance, our styles are very different. They range from funny and heartfelt to emotional and gripping. Our settings also range: from Mayfair in London to Bond Street in London, and then to, uh, Jane Street in London. Jennifer Haymore takes us to Kenilworth (80 miles from London), Courtney Milan takes us 100 miles from London to Somerset, and Sara Lindsey gets really daring and travels 120 miles to Wales. Of course, there's always Tiffany Clare, who had to show us all what's what by setting her book in Constantinople, Corfu Island, and Italy. (We love her.)

But even though selling our first books, and seeing them on the shelves for the first time has been a life-changing event, one thing hasn't changed: Our

---

[1] Maggie Robinson and Margaret Rowe are alter egos.

love for historical romance. We still send each other excited e-mails about the great books that we're reading. But now, in addition to squealing about the newest books by Elizabeth Hoyt, Liz Carlyle, and Sherry Thomas, we've added some newcomers to our stack: Tessa Dare, Maggie Robinson, Jennifer Haymore, Courtney Milan, Tiffany Clare, Margaret Rowe, and Sara Lindsey. There's no better feeling than being able to send a friend an e-mail saying, "I loved your book!"

We hope you'll give us a try—and we hope that you'll love our books, too!

Sincerely,

Tiffany Clare
Tessa Dare
Jennifer Haymore
Sara Lindsey
Courtney Milan
Maggie Robinson/Margaret Rowe

Schedule of Releases

Sara Lindsey, *Promise Me Tonight* (page 75)............................ February 2, 2010

Jennifer Haymore, *A Touch of Scandal* (page 42) .... April 1, 2010

Maggie Robinson, *Mistress by Mistake* (page 98).............................May 1, 2010

Tessa Dare, *One Dance with a Duke* (page 2) ....May 25, 2010

Sara Lindsey, *Tempting the Marquess* (page 86)............................ June 1, 2010

Margaret Rowe, *Tempting Eden* (page 118) .... June 1, 2010

Tessa Dare, *Twice Tempted by a Rogue* (page 18) .... June 22, 2010

Tessa Dare, *Three Nights with a Scoundrel* (page 19)...................... July 27, 2010

Tiffany Clare, *The Surrender of a Lady* (page 60) ....September 28, 2010

Jennifer Haymore, *A Season of Seduction* (page 50)..............September 28, 2010

Courtney Milan, *Trial by Desire* (page 22) ....September 28, 2010

Maggie Robinson, "Not Quite a Courtesan,"
   in the *Lords of Passion* Anthology (not included).......... November 30, 2010

Maggie Robinson, *Mistress by Midnight* (page 104).............. December 28, 2010

Courtney Milan, *Unveiled* (page 34).................................... February 1, 2011

Tiffany Clare, *The Seduction of his Wife*.................................. February 1, 2011

Margaret Rowe, *Any Wicked Thing* (page 123) .... March 2011

Sara Lindsey, *A Rogue for All Seasons* (not included)........................ May 2011

Jennifer Haymore's next series, The Donovan Sisters.................... May 2011

The Secret Desires of a Governess .... June 2011

Maggie Robinson, *Mistress by Marriage* (page 114) .... September 2011

Courtney Milan, *Unclaimed* (not included)...................................... Fall 2011

Tessa Dare's next series (not included) ....starts Fall 2011

Tessa Dare

Tessa Dare is a part-time librarian, full-time mommy and swing-shift writer living in Southern California.

Tessa lived a rather nomadic childhood in the Midwest. As a girl, she discovered that no matter how many times she moved, two kinds of friends traveled with her: the friends in books, and the friends in her head. She still converses with both sets daily.

Tessa writes fresh and flirty historical romance, a blog, and the stray magazine article. To the chagrin of her family, Tessa does not write grocery lists, Christmas cards, or timely checks to utility companies. She shares a tiny bungalow with her husband, their two children, a dog, and dust bunnies.

Tessa enjoys a good book, a good laugh, a good long walk in the woods, a good movie, a good meal, a glass of good wine, and the company of good people.

You can find out more about Tessa by visiting http://www.tessadare.com.

Praise for Tessa

Voted Best Debut Author of 2009, All About Romance

"Prepare to fall in love."
    –Julia Quinn, #1 *New York Times* bestselling author

"An irresistible combination of Austenesque wit and sexy romance."
    –John Charles, chicagotribune.com

" Dare seems to have fit all the best of romance into one novel."
    –*Publishers Weekly*, starred review

"The sweetest, sexiest romance you'll read all year."
    –Eloisa James, *New York Times* bestselling author

One Dance with a Duke

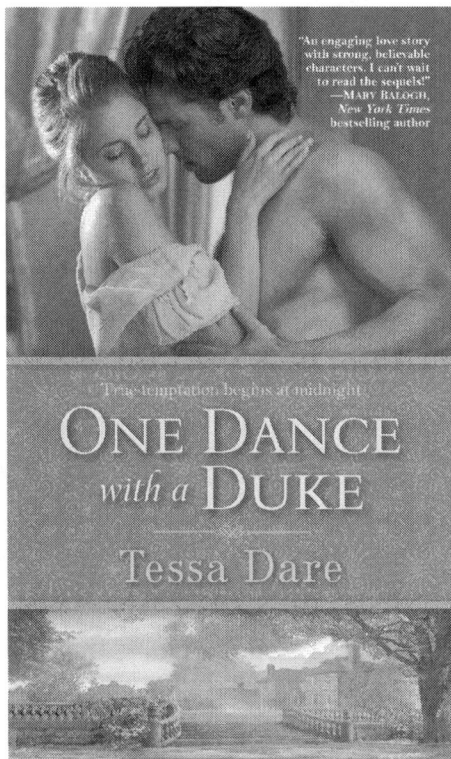

True temptation begins at midnight...

A handsome and reclusive horse breeder, Spencer Dumarque, the fourth Duke of Morland, is a member of the exclusive Stud Club, an organization so select it has only ten members—yet membership is attainable to anyone with luck. And Spencer has plenty of it, along with an obsession with a prize horse, a dark secret, and, now, a reputation as the dashing "Duke of Midnight." Each evening he selects one lady for a breathtaking midnight waltz. But none of the women catch his interest, and nobody ever bests the duke—until Lady Amelia d'Orsay tries her luck.

In a moment of desperation, the unconventional beauty claims the duke's dance and unwittingly steals his heart. When Amelia demands that Spencer forgive her scapegrace brother's debts, she never imagines that her game of wits and words will lead to breathless passion and a steamy proposal. Still, Spencer is a man of mystery, perhaps connected to the shocking murder of the Stud Club's founder. Will Amelia lose her heart in this reckless wager or win everlasting love?

Available May 25, 2010 from Ballantine Books
ISBN-10: 0345518853 ✳ ISBN-13: 978-0345518859

Chapter One

Blackberry glaze.

Biting the inside of her cheek, Amelia d'Orsay suppressed a small cry of jubilation. Even at a rout like this one, a well-bred lady's abrupt shout of joy was likely to draw notice, and Amelia did not care to explain herself to the crush of young ladies surrounding her. Especially when the reason for her delight was not a triumph at the card table or a proposal of marriage, but rather the completion of a dinner menu.

She could imagine it now. "Oh, Lady Amelia," one of these young misses would say, "only you could think of food at a time like this."

Well, it wasn't as though Amelia had *planned* to stand in a ballroom, dreaming of menus for their family summer holiday. But she'd been puzzling for weeks over a new sauce for braised pheasant, to replace the same old applejack reduction. Something sweet, yet tart; surprising, yet familiar; inventive, yet frugal. At last, the answer had come to her. Blackberry glaze. Strained, of course. Ooh, perhaps mulled with cloves.

Resolving to enter it in her menu book later, she swept the imaginary dish aside and compressed her grin to a half-smile. Summer at Briarbank would now officially be perfect.

Mrs. Bunscombe brushed past in a flounce of scarlet silk. "It's half eleven," the hostess sang. "Nearly midnight."

Nearly midnight. Now there was a thought to quell her exuberance.

A cherub-faced debutante swaddled in tulle grasped Amelia by the wrist. "Any moment now. How can you remain so calm? If he chooses me tonight, I just know I'll swoon."

Amelia sighed. And so it began. As it did at every ball, when half-eleven ticked past.

"You needn't worry about making conversation," a young lady dressed in green satin said. "He scarcely utters so much as a word."

"Are we even certain he speaks English? Wasn't he raised in Abyssinia or…"

"No, no. Lower Canada. Of course he speaks English. My brother plays cards with him." The second girl lowered her voice. "But there is something rather *primitive* about him, don't you think? I think it's the way he moves."

"I think it's the gossip you're heeding," Amelia said sensibly.

"He waltzes like a dream," a third girl put in. "When I danced with him, my feet scarcely skimmed the floor. And he's ever so handsome up close."

Amelia gave her a patient smile. "Indeed?"

At the opening of the season, the reclusive and obscenely wealthy Duke of Morland had finally entered society. A few weeks later, he had all London dancing to his tune. The duke arrived at every ball at the stroke of midnight. He selected a single partner from among the available ladies. At the conclusion of one set, he would escort the lady into supper, and then…disappear.

Before two weeks were out, the papers had dubbed him "the Duke of Midnight," and every hostess in London was jostling to invite His Grace to a ball. Unmarried ladies would not dream of promising the supper set to any other partner, for fear of missing their chance at a duke. To amplify the dramatic effect, hostesses positioned timepieces in full view, and instructed orchestras to begin the set at the very hour of twelve. And it went without saying, the set concluded with a slow, romantic waltz.

The nightly spectacle held the entire *ton* in delicious, knuckle-gnawing thrall. At every ball, the atmosphere thickened with perfume and speculation as the hour of twelve approached. It was like watching medieval knights attempting to wrest Excalibur from the stone. Surely one of these evenings, the gossips declared, some blushing ingénue would get a proper grip on the recalcitrant bachelor…and a legend would be born.

Legend indeed. There was no end of stories about him. Where a man of his rank and fortune were involved, there were always stories.

"I hear he was raised barefoot and heathen in the Canadian wilderness," said the first girl.

"I hear he was barely civilized when his uncle took him in," said the second. "And his wild behavior gave the old duke an apoplexy."

The lady in green murmured, "My brother told me there was an *incident*, at Eton. Some sort of scrape or brawl… I don't know precisely. But a boy nearly died, and Morland was expelled for it. If they sent down a duke's heir, you know it must have been dreadful."

"You'll not believe what I've heard," Amelia said, widening her eyes. The ladies perked, leaning in close. "I hear," she whispered, "that by the light of the full moon, His Grace transforms into a ravening hedgehog."

When her companions finished laughing, she said aloud, "Really, I can't believe he's so interesting as to merit this much attention."

"You wouldn't say that if *you*'d danced with him."

Amelia shook her head. She had watched this scene unfold time and again over the past few weeks, admittedly with amusement. But she never expected—or desired—to be at the center of it. It wasn't sour grapes, truly it wasn't. What other ladies saw as intriguing and romantic, she took for self-indulgent melodrama. Really, an unmarried, wealthy, handsome duke who felt the need to command *more* female attention? He must be the most vain, insufferable sort of man.

And the ladies of his choosing—all flouncy, insipid girls in their first or second seasons. All petite, all pretty. None of them anything like Amelia.

Oh, perhaps there was a hint of bitterness to it, after all.

Really, when a lady dangled on the outer cusp of marital eligibility, as she did, society ought to allow her a quiet, unannounced slide into spinsterhood. It rather galled her, to feel several years' worth of rejection revisited upon her night after night, as the infamous duke entered at the stroke of midnight, and at twelve-oh-one his eyes slid straight past her to some primping chit with more beauty than brains.

Not that he had reason to notice her. Her dowry barely scraped the floorboards of the "respectable" range, and even in her first season, she'd never been a great beauty. Her eyes were a trifle too pale, and she blushed much too easily. And at the age of six-and-twenty, she'd come to accept that she would always be a little too plump.

The girls suddenly scattered, like the flighty things they were.

A deep whisper came from behind her shoulder. "You look ravishing, Amelia."

Sighing, she wheeled to face the speaker. "Jack. What is it you're after?"

Pressing a hand to his lapel, he pulled an offended expression. "Must I be after something? Can't a fellow pay his dearest sister a compliment without falling under suspicion?"

"Not when the fellow in question is you. And it's no compliment to be called your dearest sister. I'm your only sister. If you're after my purse, you must come up with something better than that." She spoke in a light, teasing tone, hoping against all previous evidence that he would protest: *No, Amelia. This time, I'm not after your purse. I've ceased gambling and drinking, and I've thrown over those ne'er-do-well "friends" of mine. I'm returning to University. I'll take orders in the Church, just as I promised our dying mother. And you truly do look lovely tonight.*

Eyes flicking toward the crowd, he lowered his voice. "A few bob. That's all I need."

Her chest deflated. Not even midnight, and already his eyes held that wild, liquor-flared spark that indicated he was on the verge of doing something spectacularly ill-conceived.

Steering him by the elbow, she left the young ladies to titter amongst themselves and guided her brother through the nearest set of doors. They stepped into the crescent of yellow light shining through the transom window. The night air closed around them, cloying and humid.

"I don't have anything," she lied.

"A few shillings for the hack, Amelia." He grabbed for the reticule dangling from her wrist. "We're off to the theater, a gang of us."

Off to the theater, her eye. Off to the gaming hells, more likely. She clutched the beaded drawstring pouch to her bosom. "And how will I get home, then?"

"Why, Morland will take you." He winked. "Right after your dance. I've two pounds sterling on you tonight."

Wonderful. Another two pounds she'd have to siphon from her pin money. "At tremendously long odds, I'm sure."

"Don't speak like that." A touch grazed her arm. Jack's expression was suddenly, unexpectedly sincere. "He'd be damned lucky to have you, Amelia. There's no lady your equal in that room."

Tears pricked at the corners of her eyes. Since their brother Hugh's death at Waterloo, Jack had changed, and not for the better. But in rare flashes, that dear, sensitive brother she loved would surface. She wanted so desperately to gather him close and hold tight to him for weeks, months…however long it took, to coax the old Jack out from this brittle shell.

"Come now. Be a sweet sister, and lend me a crown or two. I'll send a runner to Laurent's, and he'll send that garish new landau for you. You'll be driven home in the finest style his copper heiress can afford."

"Her name is Winifred. She's the Countess of Beauvale now, and you ought to speak of her with respect. It's her fortune that purchased Michael's commission and supports young William at school. It's thanks to her and Laurent that I even have a home."

"And I'm the worthless ingrate who brings the family nothing but disgrace. I know, I know." His flinty gaze clashed with a forced smile. "It's worth a few coins to be rid of me, isn't it?"

"Can't you understand? I don't want to be rid of you at all. I love you, you fool." She smoothed that incorrigible wisp of hair that always curled at his left temple. "Won't you let me help you, Jack?"

"Of course. If you'll start with a shilling or two."

With clumsy fingers, she loosened the strings of her reticule. "I will give you everything I have, on one condition."

"What's that?"

"You must promise me you'll join us this summer, at Briarbank."

The d'Orsays always summered at Briarbank—a rambling stone cottage overlooking the River Wye, down the slope from the ruins of Beauvale Castle. Amelia had been planning this summer's holiday for months, down to the last damask tablecloth and saucer of currant jelly. Briarbank was the answer to everything, she knew it. It had to be.

Hugh's death had devastated the entire family, but Jack most of all. Of all her brothers, the two of them had been the fastest friends. Hugh had been just one year older, but several years wiser, and his serious bent had always balanced Jack's wilder personality. Without that check on his impulsive nature, Amelia feared Jack's grief and recklessness were conspiring to disaster.

What he needed was love, and time to heal. Time spent far from Town, and close to home and family—what remained of both. Here in London, Jack was surrounded by temptation, constantly pressured to keep pace with his spendthrift peers. At Briarbank, he would surely return to his good-humored self. Young William would come on his break from school. Michael would still be at sea, of course, but Laurent and Winifred would join them, at least for a week or two.

And Amelia would be the perfect hostess. Just as Mama had always been. She would fill every room with great vases of snapdragons, arrange theatricals and parlor games, serve braised pheasant with blackberry glaze.

She would make everyone happy, by sheer force of will. Or bribery, if she must.

"I've a crown and three shillings here," she said, extracting the coins from the pouch, "and six pounds more saved at home." Saved, scrimped, scraped together, one penny at a time. "It's yours, all of it—but you must promise me August at Briarbank."

Jack tsked. "He didn't tell you?"

"Who? Who didn't tell me what?"

"We're not opening the cottage this summer. It was just settled this week. We're letting it out."

"Letting it out?" Amelia felt as though all the blood had been let from her veins. Suddenly dizzy, she clutched her brother's arm. "Briarbank, let out? To strangers?"

"Well, not to strangers. We've put the word around at the clubs and expect inquiries from several good families. It's a plum holiday cottage, you know."

"Yes," she bit out. "Yes, I do know. It's so ideal, the d'Orsay family has summered there for centuries. *Centuries*, Jack. Why would we dream of leasing it out?"

"Haven't we outgrown the pall-mall and tea biscuits routine? It's dull as tombs out there. Halfway to Ireland, for God's sake."

"Dull? What on earth can you mean? You used to live for summers there, angling on the river and—" Comprehension struck, numbing her to the toes. "Oh, no." She dug her fingers into his arm. "How much did you lose? How much do you owe?"

His eyes told her he'd resigned all pretense. "Four hundred pounds."

"Four hundred! To whom?"

"To Morland."

"The Duke of Midni—" Amelia bit off the absurd nickname. She refused to puff the man's notoriety further. "But he's not even arrived yet. How did you manage to lose four hundred pounds to him, when he's not even here?"

"Not tonight. Days ago now. That's why I must leave. He'll be here any moment, and I can't face him until I've made good on the debt."

Amelia could only stare at him.

"Don't look at me like that, I can't bear it. I was holding my own until Faraday put his token in play. That's what brought Morland to the table, drove the betting sky-high. He's out to gather all ten, you know."

"All ten of what? All ten *tokens*?"

"Yes, of course. The tokens are everything." Jack made an expansive gesture. "Come now, you can't be so out of circulation as *that*. It's only the most elite gentlemen's club in London."

When she only blinked at him, he prompted, "Harcliffe. Osiris. One stud horse, ten brass tokens. You've heard of the club, I know you have."

"I'm sorry. I've no idea what you're talking about. You seem to be telling me you've wagered our ancestral home against a brass token. And lost."

"I was in for hundreds already; I couldn't back down. And my cards...Amelia, I swear to you, they were unbeatable cards."

"Except that they weren't."

He gave a fatalistic shrug. "What's done is done. If I had some other means of raising the funds, I would. I'm sorry you're disappointed, but there's always next year."

"Yes, but—" But next year was a whole year away. God only knew what trouble would find Jack in the meantime. "There must be another way. Ask Laurent for the money."

"You know he can't give it."

Of course he was right. Their eldest brother had married prudently, almost sacrificially. The family had been desperate for funds at the time, and Winifred had come with bags of money from her mining magnate father. The trouble was, the bags of money came cinched tightly with strings, and only Laurent's father-in-law could loosen them. The old man would never authorize the use of four hundred pounds to pay off a gaming debt.

"I have to leave before Morland arrives," he said. "You understand."

Jack unlooped the reticule from her limp wrist, and she did not fight him as he shook the coins into his palm. Yes, she understood. Even if nothing remained of their fortune, the d'Orsays would cling to their pride.

"Have you at least learned your lesson now?" she said quietly.

He vaulted the low terrace rail. Rattling the coins in his palm, he backed away into the garden. "You know me, Amelia. I never was any good with lessons. I just copied my slate from Hugh's."

As she watched her brother disappear into the shadows, Amelia hugged her arms across her chest.

What cruel turn of events was this? Briarbank, rented for the summer! All the happiness stored up in those cobbled floors and rustic hearths and bundles of lavender hanging from the rafters—wasted on strangers. All her elaborate menus and planned excursions, for naught. Without that cottage, the d'Orsay family had no true center. Her brother had nowhere to recover from his grief.

And somehow more lowering than all this: She had no place of her own.

Accepting spinsterhood had not been easy for Amelia. But she could resign herself to the loneliness and disappointment, she told herself, so long as she had summers at that drafty stone cottage. Those few months made the rest of the year tolerable. Whilst her friends collected lace and linens for their trousseaux, Amelia contented herself by embroidering seat covers for Briarbank. As they entertained callers, she entertained thoughts of begonias in the window box. When she—an intelligent, thoughtful, well-bred lady—was thrown over nightly for her younger, prettier, lack-witted counterparts, she could fool herself into happiness by thinking of blackberry glaze.

Lord, the irony. She wasn't much different from Jack. She'd impulsively wagered all her dreams on a pile of mortar and shale. And now she'd lost.

Alone on the terrace, she started to tremble. Destiny clanged against her hopes, beating them down one hollow ring at a time.

Somewhere inside, a clock was tolling midnight.

"His Grace, the Duke of Morland."

The majordomo's announcement coincided with the final, booming stroke of twelve.

From the head of the staircase, Spencer watched the throng of guests divide on cue, falling to either side like two halves of an overripe peach. And there, in the center, clustered the unmarried young ladies in attendance—stone-still and shriveling under his gaze.

As a general point, Spencer disliked crowds. He particularly disliked over-dressed, self-important crowds. And this scene grew more absurd by the night: the cream of London society, staring up at him with unguarded fascination.

We don't know what to make of you, those stares said.

Fair enough. It was a useful—often lucrative—thing, to be unreadable. He'd spent years cultivating the skill.

We don't trust you. This he gleaned from the whispers, and the manner in which gentlemen guarded the walls and ladies' hands instinctively went to the jewels at their throats. No matter. It also was a useful thing, at times, to be feared.

No, it was the last bit that had him quietly laughing. The silent plea that only rang louder every time he entered a ballroom.

Here, take one of our daughters.

God's knees. Must he?

As he descended the travertine staircase, Spencer girded himself for yet another unpleasant half hour. Given his preference, he would retreat back to the country and never attend another ball in his life. But while he was temporarily residing in Town, he could not refuse *all* invitations. If he wished to see his ward Claudia well-married in a few years, he must pave the way for her eventual debut. And occasionally there were high-stakes card games to be found in the back rooms of these affairs, well away from the white-powdered matrons playing whist.

So he made his appearance, but strictly on his own terms. One set, no more. As little conversation as possible. And if the *ton* were determined to throw their sacrificial virgins at his feet…he would do the choosing.

He wanted a quiet one tonight.

Usually he favored them young and vapid, more interested in preening for the crowd than capturing his notice. Then at the Pryce-Foster ball, he'd had the extreme misfortune to engage the hand of one Miss Francine Waterford. Quite pretty, with a vivacious arch to her brow and plump, rosy lips. The thing was, those lips lost all their allure when she kept them in constant motion. She'd prattled on through the entire set. Worse, she'd expected responses. While most women eagerly supplied both sides of any conversation, Miss Waterford would not be satisfied with his repertoire of brusque nods and inarticulate clearings of the throat. He'd been forced to speak at least a dozen words to her, all told.

That was his reward for indulging aesthetic sensibilities. Enough with the pretty ones. For his partner tonight, he would select a meek, silent, wallflower of a girl. She needn't be pretty, nor even passable. She need only be quiet.

As he approached the knot of young ladies, his eye settled on a slender reed of a girl standing on the fringe of the group, looking positively jaundiced in melon-colored satin. When he advanced toward her, she cowered into the shadow of her neighbor. She refused to even meet his gaze. *Perfect.*

Just as he extended his hand in invitation, he was arrested by a series of unexpected sounds. The rattle of glass panes. The slam of a door. Heels clicking against travertine in a brisk, staccato rhythm.

Spencer swiveled instinctively. A youngish woman in blue careened across the floor like a billiard ball, reeling to a halt before him. His hand remained outstretched from his aborted invitation to Miss Melony Satin, and this newly-arrived lady took hold of it firmly.

Dipping in a shallow curtsey, she said, "Thank you, Your Grace. I would be honored."

And after a stunned, painful pause, the music began.

The clump of disappointed ladies dispersed in search of new partners, grumbling as they went. And for the first time all season, Spencer found himself partnered with a lady not of his choosing. *She* had selected *him.*

How very surprising.

How very unpleasant.

Nevertheless, there was nothing to be done. The impertinent woman queued up across from him for the country dance. Did he even know this lady?

As the other dancers fell into place around them, he took the opportunity to study her. He found little to admire. Any measure of genteel poise she might claim had fallen casualty to that inelegant sprint across the ballroom. Stray wisps of hair floated about her face; her breath was labored with exertion. This state of agitation did her complexion no favors, but it did enhance the swell of her ample bosom. She was amply endowed everywhere, actually. Generous curves pulled against the blue silk of her gown.

"Forgive me," he said, as they circled one another. "Have we been introduced?"

"Years ago, once. I would not expect you to remember. I am Lady Amelia d'Orsay."

The pattern of the dance parted them, and Spencer had some moments to absorb this name: Lady Amelia d'Orsay. Her late father had been the seventh Earl of Beauvale. Her elder brother, Laurent, was currently the eighth Earl of Beauvale.

And her younger brother Jack was a scapegrace wastrel who owed Spencer four hundred pounds.

She must have sensed the moment of this epiphany, for when they next clasped hands she said, "We needn't speak of it now. It can wait for the waltz."

He quietly groaned. This was going to be a very long set. If only he'd moved more quickly in securing the jaundiced one's hand. Now that Lady Amelia's brash maneuver had been successful, God only knew what stunt the ladies—or more likely, their mothers—would attempt next. Maybe he should start engaging his partners' hands in advance of the event. But that would necessitate social calls, and Spencer did not make social calls. Perhaps he could direct his secretary to send notes? The entire situation was wearying.

The country dance ended. The waltz began. And he was forced to take her in his arms, this woman who had just made his life a great deal more complicated.

To her credit, she wasted no time with pleasantries. "Your Grace, let me be to the point. My brother owes you a great sum of money."

"He owes me four hundred pounds."

"Do you not view that as a great sum of money?"

"I view it as a debt which I am owed. The precise amount is inconsequential."

"It is not inconsequential to me. I cannot imagine that you are unaware of it, but the d'Orsay name is synonymous with noble poverty. For us, four hundred pounds is a vast sum of money. We simply cannot spare it."

"And what do you propose? Do you mean to offer me favors in lieu of payment?" He repaid her shocked expression with a cool remark: "I'm not interested."

It was a small lie. He was a man. And she was a buxom woman, poured into a form-fitting dress. Parts of him were finding parts of her vaguely interesting. His eyes, for example, kept straying to her décolletage, so snugly framed by blue silk and ivory lace. From his advantage of height, he could spy the dark freckle dotting the inner curve of her left breast, and time and again, he found his gaze straying to the small imperfection.

"What a revolting suggestion," she said. "Do you routinely solicit such offers from the distraught female relations of your debtors?"

He gave a noncommittal shrug. He didn't, but she was free to believe he did. Spencer was not in the habit of ingratiating himself, with anyone.

"As if I would barter my favors for four hundred pounds."

"I thought you called it a vast sum of money." *Well above the going rate for such services*, he refrained from adding.

"There are some things upon which one cannot put a price."

He considered making an academic argument to the contrary, but decided against it. Clearly the woman lacked the sense to follow logic. As was further evidenced by her next comment.

"I ask you to forgive Jack's debt."

"I refuse."

"You cannot refuse!"

"I just did."

"Four hundred pounds is nothing to you. Come now, you weren't even after Jack's money. He was only caught in the middle as you drove the betting high. You wanted Mr. Faraday's token, and you have it. Let my brother's wager be set aside."

"No."

She huffed an impatient breath, and her whole body seemed to exhale in exasperation. Frustration exuded from her every pore, and with it wafted her own unique feminine scent. She smelled nice, actually. No cloying perfume— he supposed she couldn't afford rich scent. Just the common aromas of plain soap and clean skin, and the merest suggestion that she tucked sprigs of lavender between her stored undergarments.

Blue eyes locked with his. "Why not?"

Spencer tempered his own exasperated sigh. He could explain to her that forgiving the debt would do both her brother and her family a great disservice. They would owe a debt of gratitude more lasting and burdensome than any debt of gold, impossible to repay. Worst, Jack would have no incentive to avoid repeating the mistake. In a matter of weeks, the youth would land in even deeper debt, perhaps to the tune of thousands. Spencer had no doubt that four hundred pounds was a large sum to the d'Orsay family, but it would not be a crippling one. And if it purchased Lady Amelia's brother a greater portion of sense, it would be four hundred pounds well spent.

All this he might have explained. But he was the Duke of Morland. As much as he'd forfeited for the sake of that title, it ought to come with a few advantages. He shouldn't have to explain himself at all.

"Because I won't," he said simply.

She set her teeth. "I see. And there is nothing I can say to persuade you otherwise?"

"No."

Lady Amelia shuddered. He felt the tremor beneath his palm, where his hand pressed against the small of her back. Fearing she might burst out weeping—and wouldn't *that* be the final polish on this sterling example of awkwardness—Spencer pulled her tightly to him and whisked her into a series of turns.

Despite his efforts, she only trembled more violently. Small sounds, something between a hiccough and a squeak, emanated from her throat. Against his better judgment, he pulled back to study her face.

The woman was laughing.

His heart began to beat a little faster. *Steady, man.*

"It is true, what the ladies say. You do waltz like a dream." Her eyes swept his face, catching on his brow, his jaw, and finally fixing on his mouth with unabashed interest. "And you are undeniably handsome, up close."

"Do you hope to move me by means of flattery? It won't work."

"No, no." She smiled, and her right cheek dimpled. The left did not. "I see now that you are a positively immutable gentleman, a veritable rock of determination, and my every attempt to move you would be in vain."

"Why the laughter, then?"

Why the question? he berated himself, annoyed. Why not gratefully allow to the conversation to die? And why did he find himself wondering whether Lady Amelia's left cheek ever dimpled? Whether she smiled more genuinely, more freely in situations that did not involve debasing herself over large debts, or whether the lone dimple was merely another of her intrinsic imperfections, like the unmatched freckle on her breast?

"Because," she answered, "anxiety and gloom are tiresome. You've made it clear you will not forgive the debt. I can pass the remainder of the set moping about it, or I can enjoy myself."

"*Enjoy* yourself."

"The notion shocks you, I see. I know there are some"—here she raked him with a sharp glance—"who judge it mark of their superiority to always appear dissatisfied with the available company. Before they even enter a gathering, they have made up their minds to be displeased with it. Is it so very unthinkable that I might choose the reverse? Opt for happiness, even in the face of grave personal disappointment and complete financial ruin?"

"It smacks of insincerity."

"Insincerity?" She laughed again. "Forgive me, but are you not the Duke of Morland? The playwright of this little midnight melodrama that has played to packed houses for weeks? The entire scene is predicated on the assumption that we eligible ladies are positively desperate to catch your attention. That a dance in the Duke of Midnight's arms is every girl's fondest fantasy. And now you call me insincere, when I claim to be enjoying my turn?"

She lifted her chin and looked out over the ballroom. "I have no illusions about myself. I'm an impoverished gentlewoman, two seasons on the shelf, no great beauty even in my bloom of youth. I'm not often at the center of attention, Your Grace. When this waltz concludes, I don't know when—if ever—I shall know the feeling again. So I'm determined to enjoy it while it lasts." She smiled fiercely, defiantly. "And you can't stop me."

Spencer concluded this must now be the longest set in the history of dancing. Turning his head, he dutifully swept her the length of the floor, striving to ignore how every pair of eyes in the ballroom tracked their progress. Quite a crowd tonight.

When he risked a glance down at her, Lady Amelia's face remained tilted to his.

"Can I persuade you to stop staring at me?"

Her smile never faltered. "Oh, no."

Oh no, indeed.

"You see," she whispered in a husky tone, that from any other woman he would have interpreted as sensual overture, "it's not often a spinster like me has the opportunity to enjoy such a prime specimen of virility and vigor, and at such close proximity. Those piercing hazel eyes, and all that dark, curling hair... What a struggle it is, not to touch it."

He shushed her. "You're creating a scene."

"Oh, you created the scene," she murmured coyly. "I'm merely stealing it."

Would this waltz never end?

"Did you wish to change the subject?" she asked. "Perhaps we should speak of the theater."

"I don't go to the theater."

"Books, then. How about books?"

"Some other time," he ground out. And instantly wondered what had possessed him to say *that*. The odd thing of it was, despite her many, many unpleasant attributes, Lady Amelia was clearly possessed of some intelligence and wit. He could not help but think that in another time, in another place, he might have enjoyed discussing books with her. But he couldn't possibly do so here, in a crowded ballroom, with his concentration unraveling on each successive twirl.

His control of the scene was slipping.

And that made him frown.

"Ooh, that's a dangerous glare," she said. "And your face is turning a most impressive shade of red. It's enough to make me believe all those dreadful rumors about you. Why, you're actually raising the hairs on my neck."

"Stop this."

"I am all honesty," she protested. "See for yourself." She stretched up and tilted her head to the side, elongating the smooth, pale column of her neck. No freckles there. Only an enticing curve of creamy, soft-looking, sweet-smelling female skin.

Now Spencer's heart slammed against his ribs. He didn't know which he yearned to do more. Wring that neck, or lick it. Biting it might be a fair compromise. An action that mingled pleasure with punishment.

Because she deserved to be punished, the impertinent minx. Accepting the futility of her first argument, she'd chosen to wage a different battle. A rebellion of joy. *I may not wrest a penny from you, but I will wring every possible drop of enjoyment at your expense.*

This was the very attitude responsible for her brother's debt. Jack would not quit the card table, even when he had no hope of recouping his losses. He stayed in, risked hundreds he did not have, because he wanted to win one last hand. It was precisely the temperament one might expect from a family such as the d'Orsays—a lineage rich with centuries of pride and valor, perpetually strapped for gold.

Lady Amelia wanted to best him at something. She wanted to see him brought low. And through no particular skill or perception of her own, she was perilously close to succeeding.

Spencer came to an abrupt halt. Implausibly, the room kept spinning around him. Damn it, this couldn't be happening. Not here, not now.

But the signs were unmistakable. His pulse pounded in his ears. A wave of heat swamped his body. The air was suddenly thick as treacle, and tasted just as vile.

Devil, damn, blast. He needed to leave this place, immediately.

"Why have we stopped?" she said. "The waltz isn't over." Her voice sounded as though it came from a great distance, filtered through cotton-wool.

"It's over for me." Spencer swung his gaze around the room. An open set of doors to his left beckoned promisingly. He attempted to release her, but she clutched at his shoulders and held him fast. "For God's sake," he said, "let me—"

"Let you what?" Her eyes darting to the side, she whispered, "Let you go? Let you abandon me here on the dance floor, to my complete and total humiliation? Of all the unchivalrous, ungentlemanly, unforgivable…" When she ran out of descriptors, she threw him an accusatory glare that implied a thousand more. "I won't stand for it."

"Very well, then. Don't."

He slid his hands to her waist, grasped tight with both hands, and bodily lifted Lady Amelia d'Orsay—two, four…six inches off the floor. Until they looked one another eye-to-eye, and her slippers dangled in mid-air.

He spared a brief moment to savor the way indignant shock widened those pale blue eyes.

And then he carried her out into the night.

Twice Tempted by a Rogue

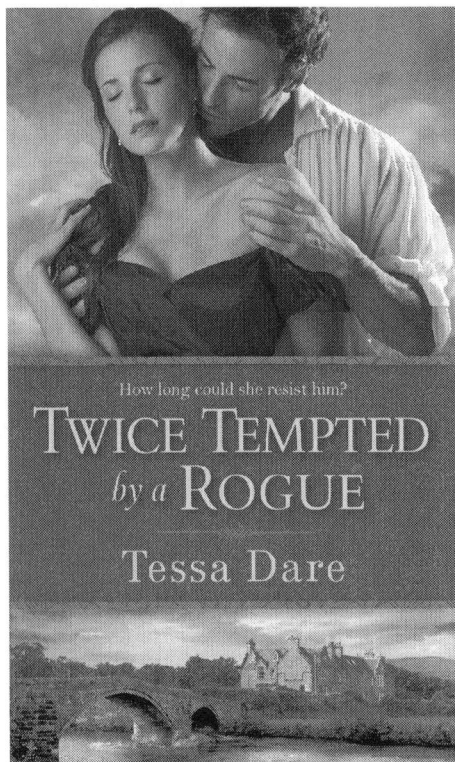

How long could she resist him?

Luck is a double-edged sword for brooding war hero Rhys St. Maur. His death wish went unanswered on the battlefield, while fate allowed the murder of his friend in the elite gentlemen's society known as the Stud Club. Out of options, Rhys returns to his ancestral home on the moors of Devonshire, expecting anything but a chance at redemption in the arms of a beautiful innkeeper, who dares him to take on the demons of his past — and the sweet temptation of a woman's love.

Meredith Maddox believes in hard work, not fate, and romance isn't part of her plan. But when Rhys returns, battle-scarred, world-weary, and more dangerously attractive than ever, the lovely widow is torn between determination and desire. As a deep mystery and dangerous smugglers threaten much more than their passionate reckoning, Meredith discovers that she must trust everything to a wager her heart placed long ago.

Available June 22, 2010 from Ballantine Books
ISBN-10: 034551887X ✳*ISBN-13: 978-0345518873*

Three Nights with a Scoundrel

The third time is the charm.

The bastard son of a nobleman, Julian Bellamy is now polished to perfection, enthralling the *ton* with wit and charm while clandestinely plotting to ruin the lords, ravish the ladies, and have the last laugh on a society that once spurned him. But meeting Leo Chatwick, a decent man and founder of the exclusive Stud Club, and Lily, Leo's enchanting sister, made Julian reconsider his wild ways. When Leo's tragic murder demands that Julian hunt for justice, he vows to see the woman he secretly loves married to a man of her own class.

Lily, however, has a very different husband in mind. She's adored Julian forever, loves the man beneath the rakish facade, and wants to savor the delicious attraction they share—as his wife. His insistence on marrying her off only reinforces her intent to prove he is the only man for her. Obsessed with catching a killer, Julian sinks back to the gutters of his youth, forcing Lily to reach out with a sweet, reckless passion Julian can't resist. Can her desire for a scoundrel save them both—or will dangerous secrets threaten more than their tender love?

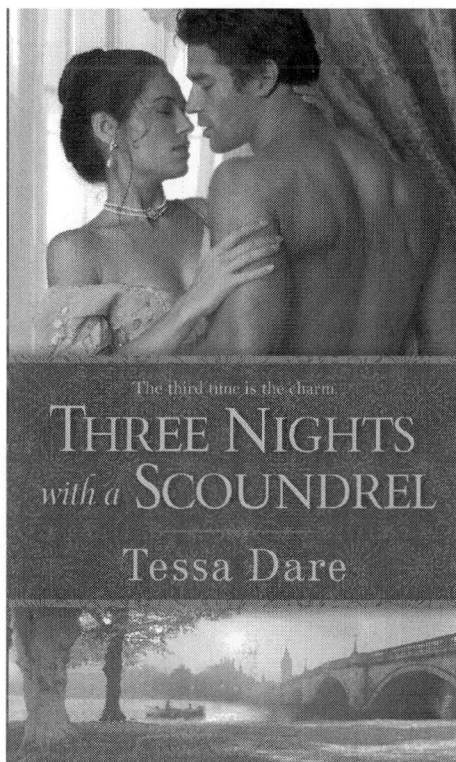

Available July 27, 2010 from Ballantine Books
ISBN-10: 0345518896 ✳*ISBN-13: 978-034551889*

Still Available

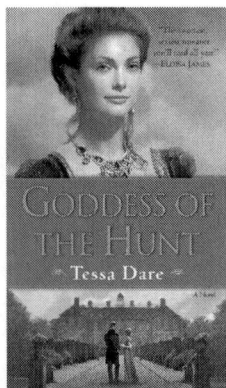

Goddess of the Hunt
ISBN-10: 0345506863 ✻ *ISBN-13: 978-0345506863*

Best First Historical Romance,
  RT Book Reviewer's Choice Awards

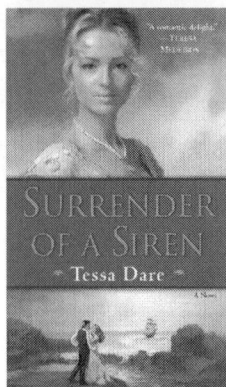

Surrender of a Siren
ISBN-10: 0345506871 ✻ *ISBN-13: 978-0345506870*

2010 RITA® Award Finalist

"Filled with adventure, three-dimensional characters and exciting plots, yet she maintains the purest form of romance."
  —*RT Book Reviews*, 4½ stars, TOP Pick!

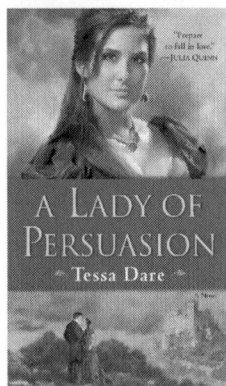

A Lady of Persuasion
ISBN-10: 034550688X ✻ ISBN-13: 978-0345506887

"Wry wit, endearing characters, laugh-out-loud moments, sensual interludes and poignancy. This is stellar storytelling!"
  —*RT Book Reviews*, 4½ stars, TOP Pick!

Courtney Milan

Courtney Milan lives in the Pacific Northwest with her husband, a well-trained dog, and an attack cat. Courtney wishes she could say she has lived in numerous fabulous places. But aside from her husband, there is a distinct lack of fabulousness in her life. Instead, she is happy when standards in the Milan household hover above mediocrity. Her husband attempts not to kill people for a living.[2] In exchange, Courtney attempts not to do the dishes.

Before she started writing historical romance, Courtney experimented with various occupations: computer programming, dog-training, scientificating. . . . Having given up on being able to *do* any of those things, she's taken to heart the axiom that those who can't do, teach. When she's not reading (lots), writing (lots), or sleeping (not enough), she can be found in the vicinity of a classroom.

You can find out more about Courtney by visiting http://www.courtneymilan.com.

Praise for Courtney

"Milan's powerhouse debut… comes with a full complement of humor, characterization, plot and sheer gutsiness."
    —Publishers' Weekly, starred review

"A dazzling debut by a multitalented author… Completely satisfying, this is a book meant for all time."
    —RT Book Reviews magazine

"Mix in captivating secondary characters, lively writing, and sexy chemistry, and the result is an unforgettable romance debut."
    —John Charles, *Booklist*

---

[2] The astute reader will notice that this sentence can be read as either "Courtney's husband attempts to make his living by means other than offing unsuspecting passersby," or as "Courtney's husband, while making a living, tries not to leave dead bodies in his wake." Luckily, both are true, although it must be admitted that Mr. Milan has had greater success with the former.

Trial by Desire

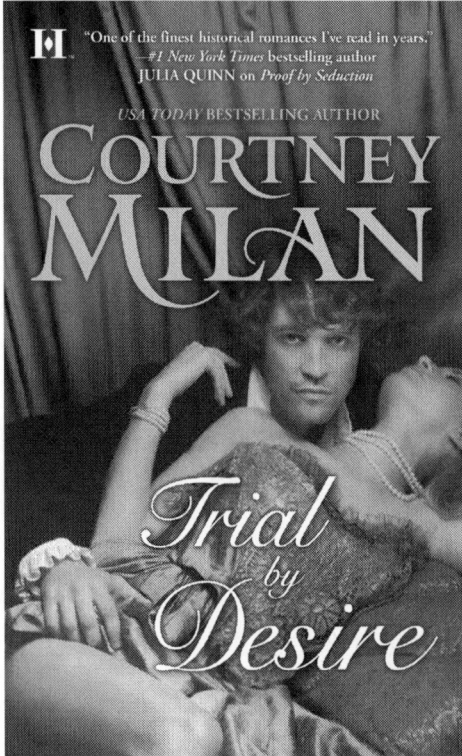

"One of the finest historical romances I've read in years."
—*#1 New York Times* bestselling author
JULIA QUINN on *Proof by Seduction*

USA TODAY BESTSELLING AUTHOR

COURTNEY MILAN

Trial by Desire

She cannot forget the fire he ignited…

In the three years since her husband left her, Lady Kathleen Carhart has managed to forge a fulfilling life for herself. But when Ned Carhart unexpectedly returns, she finds her tranquility uprooted—and her deepest secrets threatened. Though she has no intention of falling for Ned's charms, Kate can no longer deny the desire that still burns in her heart.

Or the promise of his love.

Ned is determined to regain his wife's trust by using unbridled seduction. But just as Kate surrenders to Ned's passion, her carefully guarded past threatens to destroy her. Now Kate must place her faith in the only man she's ever loved, and the only one who has ever betrayed her…

Available September 28, 2010 from HQN Books
ISBN-10: 0373774850 ✳*ISBN-13: 978-037377485*

Chapter One

A shoulder-high wall hugged the dirt road that wound its way up the hill Kate was climbing. Last night, when she and the nursemaid had crept by on foot, the dark stones of the wall had seemed menacing, hunched things. She'd imagined Eustace Paxton, the Earl of Harcroft, crouching behind every rock, ready to spit vile curses at her.

But through the diffuse morning fog, she could make out little yellow-headed wildflowers growing between the rocks. Even this aging edifice had become friendly and bright. And Harcroft was thirty miles away, in London, unaware of her involvement in his latest misfortunes. She'd won a respite, and for the first time in two weeks, she breathed easily.

As if to belie her certainty, the plod of horse hooves carried to her on a breeze. She turned, her heart accelerating. Despite the flush of heat that rose in her, Kate clutched her heavy cloak about her. She'd been discovered. He was here—

There was nothing behind her but morning mist. She was imagining things, to think that Harcroft would have uncovered her secret so quickly. She let out a covert breath—and then gulped it back as the creak of wooden wheels sounded once more. This time, though, it was clear the noise came from up the road. As she peered ahead of her, the dark form of a cart, lumbering up the hill, resolved in the mist.

The sight was as calming as it was familiar. A blanket of fog had obscured the sound's origin. The cart moved slowly, drawn by a single animal. As Kate trudged up the hill, her calves burning with the exertion, she made out more details. The conveyance was filled with heavy wooden kegs, marked with a sigil she could not make out from here. The animal that pulled this cargo seemed some nondescript color, unidentifiable in the mist. From this distance, its coat appeared to be both spotted and striped with light gray. It strained uphill, bone and muscle rippling underneath that oddly-colored pelt.

Kate sighed with relief. The man was a common laborer. Not Harcroft; therefore, not someone who posed a threat, if he discovered the role she'd played last night. Still, Kate pulled her hood up to shield her face. The scratchy wool was the only disguise she had.

As if in reminder of the nightmare that Louisa had escaped, a whip-crack sounded in front of her. Kate gritted her teeth and continued up the hill. Half a minute later, and a number of yards closer, the whip cracked again. She bit her tongue.

She had to be practical. Lady Kathleen Carhart might have had sharp words for the man. But right now, Kate was wrapped in an ill-fitting cloak, and the servant she was pretending to be would keep her eyes downcast. A servant would never speak up, not to a man with a horse and a whip. He would never believe her the lady of the manor, not dressed as she was.

And besides, the last thing Kate needed if she intended to keep her secrets was for society to hear that she'd been skulking about, dressed as a servant. As she climbed the hill, the lash continued to fall. She gritted her teeth in fury as she drew abreast of the cart. Perhaps that was why, at first, she didn't hear it.

Above the complaining rumble of the cartwheels, the noise had been at first indiscernible. But the wind shifted, and with it, brought the rhythmic sound of a gentle canter to her ears.

Kate glanced behind her. A horseman was coming up the hill.

A simple carter might once have caught a glimpse of Lady Kathleen at a harvest festival—a close enough look to boast, over a tankard of ale, perhaps, about seeing a duke's daughter. He wouldn't recognize her when she was swathed in a heavy cloak and a working woman's bonnet.

But a man on horseback could be a gentleman. He might, in fact, be the Earl of Harcroft, come looking for his missing wife. And if Harcroft came upon Kate dressed in this fashion—if he *recognized* her—he might guess the role she'd played in his wife's disappearance.

All he would have to do was trace her path back a few miles. That shepherd's cottage wasn't so very far away.

Kate pulled the hood of her cloak farther over her eyes and slunk closer to the wall. Her hand brushed against grit on its uneven surface. Even though she huddled in her cloak, she set her chin. She was not about to surrender Louisa to her husband. No matter what he said or did.

The man on horseback came into view through the mist just as Kate crested the hill. Shreds of fog splashed around his horse's hooves, like gray, slow-moving seawater. The horse was a gentleman's beast: a slim mare, gray as the wisps of vapor that clung to its legs. *Not* Harcroft's chestnut stallion, then. Reassured, Kate studied the gentleman himself.

He wore a tall hat and a long coat; the tails flapped behind him, in rhythmic counterpoint to the fall of his mare's hooves. Whoever he was, his shoulders were too broad to belong to Harcroft. Besides, this man's face was covered by a sandy beard. *Definitely* not Harcroft, then. Not any man she recognized.

That didn't mean he wouldn't recognize her, or that he wouldn't carry stories.

Slowly, she let out her breath and turned to look forward. If she didn't draw attention to herself, he wouldn't notice her. She looked like a servant; she would be virtually invisible to a man of his class.

The mare's light hoofbeats pattered up the hill. It moved in effortless contrast to the other poor animal, which was still dragging its Sisyphean burden to the summit. Kate had her own burdens to think of. Out of the corner of her eye, she saw the horseman pull ahead of the cart. The tails of his coat flapped briefly across the beast's blinkered vision. A foot or so of fabric; nothing more.

The horse pulling the cart, however, stopped and shied, pinning its ears against its head in a gesture of equine distress. Kate pressed against the wall as the cart's wooden shafts creaked. Another flap of the coattails in the wind; when the whip cracked again, Kate winced. The carter's horse did more than that: It let out a frightened cry and reared up on its hind legs. The cart tilted precariously; the hooves thundered down. Kate heard the crashing splinter of wood, and she whirled to face the animal.

One of the cart shafts had split down the middle. The horse was tangled in halter and traces, and no matter how it strained, it could not escape. When frightened, horses ran; and when they couldn't run—

Kate caught a glimpse of a dark eye rolled back, ears flattened against the long head. The horse's blinkered gaze momentarily fixed on hers. *Crack* went the whip, and the horse reared in response. It was so close, Kate could see its iron shoes as it pawed the air above her head. She felt frozen in that moment, as useless as a rabbit cowering in the grass with a hawk plummeting down. Her hands went cold. Her mind moved sluggishly. She might have counted the horse's ribs, every prominent ridge, as the hooves descended towards her.

And then the moment of fear passed, and practical considerations overtook her disbelief.

She dropped to the ground in a crouch, just as those massive hooves hit the crumbling wall where her head had been. Once, and bits of stone and crumbling grout rained on her head; twice, and flying chips of rock struck her cheek. The animal whinnied and reared again.

Before the hooves could land a third time, someone stepped in front of her. Whoever it was jerked her to her feet—the sockets of her arms twinged in protest. His body pressed against hers momentarily, a brief imprint of hard muscle fitting against her curves. He turned his back to the beast, shielding her from those iron-clad hooves. It was the horseman—the gentleman on the gray mare. He must have dismounted and come to offer assistance.

She had no chance to protest, even had she wanted to, no opportunity to pull away. His hands clasped her waist, and he lifted her up, up, until her palms scrabbled along the top of the wall behind her. She pulled herself atop it, heart thumping, and glanced down. The horseman was looking up at her. His eyes, liquid brown pools, sparkled at her over that shaggy beard, as if this were the best excitement he'd come upon in weeks. For one instant, she felt a sick thrill of recognition.

I know this man.

But he turned away, and that feeling of familiarity slipped through her fingers, as hard to hold on to as the gritty pebbles on the wall she clung to.

Whoever he was, he had no notion of fear. He turned back to the careening beast. He moved on his toes with a graceful economy of motion. It was almost as if he were leading the horse in a waltz. The man sidestepped another furious stamp of those hooves.

"There now, Champion." His voice was quiet but carrying. "I don't *want* to crowd you so closely, but you'll never calm down if I can't cut the traces."

"Cut the traces!" protested the carter, clutching the handle of his whip. "What the devil do you mean, *cut the traces?*"

The gentleman paid him no mind. Instead, he made a half-turn, and stepped behind the animal.

The carter held his whip back, his mouth pursed in ugly disapproval. "What in blazes do you think you're doing?"

The gentleman turned his back on the furious driver. He was talking—murmuring, actually. Kate couldn't hear his words, but she could catch the tone of his voice, soft and soothing. The beast pawed the air once more, and then danced from hoof to hoof. It whipped its head to the side, trying to keep its eyes on the gentleman behind it. A swipe with his knife, then another; one final adjustment of leather, and the animal came free of the cart.

"What the devil are you doing? That's my animal you're freeing, it is!"

The horse surged forward. The carter still held the reins in one hand, and so it couldn't bolt far. But without the bits of cart swinging around it—and more importantly, with the carter left to impotently clutch his whip now that the beast was out of range—the horse pranced, pawed the ground in distress once, and then, eying the people around it, lapsed into a restive silence.

"There," the gentleman said, "that's better, isn't it?"

And like that, it *was* better. All the other sounds of the autumn morning seemed to resume with his words: the thump of Kate's heart, the horse's uneasy stamp on the road below her; the impatient sound of the carter beating the handle of his whip against his other hand. She clutched the wall beneath her.

"You gentlemen are all alike. You're coddling it," the carter complained. "Stupid animal."

The last was directed at the horse, which still trembled despite the so-called coddling, its ears flat against the sides of its head. The bearded gentleman—and by the cultured drawl of his voice and the fashionable cut of his coat, he was surely a gentleman—turned to face the carter. He walked towards him and then reached down and gathered the animal's reins in his hand. The carter relinquished them, staring in front of him in stupefaction.

"Coddling?" the fellow said gently. "Champion here is an animal, not an egg. Besides, I make it a point to be kind to beasts that are large enough to stomp me to bits. Particularly when they are frightened enough to do so. I've always thought it foolish to stand on principle, when the principle is about to trample you to death."

That evanescent sense of familiarity came to her again, troubling as an unidentified smell on the wind. Something in his voice reminded her of something, *someone*—but no, she would remember that tone of quiet command if ever she'd heard it.

Kate took another deep breath—and froze. She'd only seen the beast in sidelong glances up until now. In the fog, that strange coloration, those odd white spots, had seemed as if they were some curious form of natural marking. But from her vantage point atop the wall, she could see the marks for what they were: scars. Scars where a whip had drawn blood; scars where an ill-fitting harness had rubbed over the course of who knew how many years.

No wonder the poor animal had rebelled.

The carter was holding his hands out. "Here now," he complained. "It don't hurt him. My mam always used to say that tribulation was sent to make you stronger. It's in the Bible. I think." The carter trailed off, giving the horseman a hapless shrug.

"How curious." The fellow smiled disarmingly; even through that thick beard, his grin was infectious, and the carter echoed it with a gap-toothed smile. "I cannot recall the commandment to beat animals. But then, I disagree with the premise. In my experience, tribulation doesn't strengthen you. It's more like to leave you with a bronchial inflammation that lingers for years."

"Pardon?"

The gentleman waved a hand and turned back to the animal. "Never trust aphorisms. Any sentiment short enough to be memorable is undoubtedly wrong."

Kate suppressed a smile. As if the gentleman could see her, his lips twitched upward. Of course, focused as he was on the trembling cart-horse, she doubted he even knew she was still here. Slowly, she slid from the wall to the ground.

The gentleman fished in his pockets and pulled out an apple. The animal's nostrils widened; its ears came forward slightly. Kate could see its ribs. They were not prominent enough to indicate starvation, but neither were they covered with a healthy amount of skin and muscle. Underneath those healed lacerations, its coat might once have been chestnut. But coal dust and road mud, stretched over scarred skin, had robbed the pelt of any hint of gloss.

"Oh, don't *feed* it, for the love of all that is precious," the carter protested. "The beast is useless. I've had it for three months, and no matter how I beat it, still it shies away from every last mother-loving noise."

"That," said the gentleman, "sounds like an explanation, rather than an excuse. Doesn't it, Champion?" He tossed the apple on the ground next to the horse and then looked away into the distance.

He seemed good with the beast. Gentle. Kind. Not that it mattered, because whoever he was, she couldn't speak to him. No matter how kind he was, he couldn't know what Lady Kathleen had been doing, not if she intended to keep her secrets safe. Kate began to sidle away from the scene.

"Champion? Who're you calling Champion?"

"Well, has he got another name?" The man had made no move to get closer to the horse. He stood a reins' distance from the beast, looking away from the valley. Towards Berkswift, actually. Kate's home, just beyond one last rise and a row of trees.

"Name?" The carter frowned, as if the very concept were foreign. "I've been calling it *Meat*."

"Meet?" The gentleman frowned down at the reins gathered in his hands. "As in a championship meet? A tourney?"

"No. *Meat*. As in, *Horse Meat*. As in, I could get a ha'penny per stringy pound from the butcher."

The gentleman's fingers curled about the reins. "I'll give you ten pounds for the whole animal."

"Ten pounds? Why, that's barely what the knacker—"

"If *Meat* here panics on the way to the knacker, you'll be out far more than that in property damage." The man glanced at Kate, where she'd been sneaking away from the battered cart.

It was the first time he'd looked at her directly, and Kate felt his gaze settle against her, disturbing and familiar all at once. She pressed against the wall.

The gentleman simply shook his head and looked away. "You should be brought up on criminal charges, for endangerment." He reached into his pocket, produced a small purse, and began to count coins.

"Here now. I haven't agreed. How am I supposed to move my cart?"

The gentleman shrugged. "With that shaft broken? I don't imagine a horse would prove much help." But as he spoke, he added a few more coins from his purse and then dropped them on the cart driver's seat. "There's a village yonder."

The carter shook his head and collected the pile. Then, he stood and left his cart, trudging on towards the village. The gentleman watched him go.

While the man was still distracted, Kate began to walk away. The horse was safe, and if she left now, her secret—*Louisa*'s secret—was safe, too. Whoever this man was, he couldn't have recognized her. No doubt he thought her some servant, off on her mistress's errands. An unimportant thing, as nondescript as the beast he'd rescued.

He touched his hat at her, and then turned back to his own manicured steed, which waited in nonchalant obedience ten yards down the track.

Kate had supposed the newly-purchased beast would follow docilely in the gentleman's footsteps, beaten-down specimen that it was. But it did not hang its head; instead as the fellow led it back to where he'd loosely tossed the reins of his steed, Horse Meat tossed its ragged mane. It lifted one lip in disdain and stamped its bone-thin, lacerated legs.

The gray mare ducked its head and backed away a step.

"Do you suppose they'll walk calmly together?" the gentleman asked.

With the carter gone, there was nobody else around. He had to be addressing her.

Kate glanced at him, in the midst of her escape. She didn't dare speak. Her voice would betray her as a lady, even if her clothing hadn't. She shook her head.

Horse Meat curled its lips at the mare, showing teeth. It could not have communicated more clearly, had it spoken: *Stay away from me. I am a dangerous stallion!*

The gentleman looked from animal to animal. "I suppose not." A soft smile of bemusement passed over his lips, and he turned to meet Kate's eyes, once again halting her forward progress.

There was a restless vitality about those eyes that resonated with her. Something about him—his voice, his easy confidence—set her skin humming in recognition. She knew him.

Or maybe she just wanted to know him, and she'd invented this subtle sense of familiarity. She would have remembered a man like him.

Unlike other gentlemen, underneath his hat, his skin was sun-warmed gold. His shoulders were broad, and not by any artifice of padding. He was walking away from his steed, towards Kate.

No, she couldn't *possibly* have forgotten a man like him. His gaze on her made her feel uneasy, as if he knew all her secrets. As if he were laughing at every last one.

"Well," he said, "this is a pretty pickle, my lady."

My lady? Ladies did not wear itchy gray cloaks. They didn't cower under shapeless bonnets. Had he seen the fine walking dress she wore underneath when he lifted her up? Or did he know who she was?

His eyes flicked up and down, once, an automatic, male survey of her figure, before returning to her face.

Kate was not fool enough to wish he'd let the horse trample her. Still, she wished he'd been on his way earlier. At least he didn't remark on her outlandish garb. Instead...

"This," he told her, gesturing with the reins of the animal he'd just acquired, "puts me in mind of one of those damnable logic puzzles a friend of mine used to pose when we were at Cambridge. 'A shepherd, three sheep, and a wolf must cross a river in a boat that fits at most two....'"

Understanding—and disappointment—took root. No wonder he wasn't courting her ire by asking inconvenient questions about her cloak and her lack of companionship. He was one of *those* men. He addressed her with easy intimacy. A tone of expectation warmed his voice, entirely at odds with his formal "my lady." She recalled his hands on her waist, that brief flash of heated contact, body to body. At the time, she'd noticed nothing more than a fleeting impression of hard muscle pushing her out of harm's way. Now, her skin prickled where he'd touched her, as if his gaze had sparked her flesh to life.

If he knew her well enough to attempt to win that wager, then he knew her well enough to gossip. He knew her well enough to spread the word in town, and well enough for that word to travel round until it reached Harcroft's ears. It was no longer a question of *if* Harcroft would hear about this episode; it was a matter of *what* and *when*.

Kate didn't dare panic, not now. She took a deep breath. She needed to make sure that the crux of his story had nothing to do with the clothing in which he found her.

"This isn't the time for games of logic," she said. "You know who I am."

He stared at her in befuddlement. One hand rose to touch his chin, and he shook his head. "Of course I know who you are. I knew who you were the instant I set my hands on your hips."

No true gentleman would have alluded to that uncouth contact. But then, no true gentleman would make her want to wrap her arms around her own waist, to press her palms where his had been before.

She cast him a brilliant smile, and after a moment, he responded with a like expression. She crooked her index finger at him, and he took a step towards her.

"You're thinking about that bet, aren't you?"

He stopped in his tracks and shook his head stupidly—but all that false bewilderment could not fool Kate. She'd seen too many variants upon it over the years.

"It's been on the book for two years now," Kate said. "Of *course* you're thinking of it. And you"—here, she extended her gloved hand to point playfully at his chest—"*you* have convinced yourself that you will be the one to claim the five thousand pounds."

His brows drew down.

"Oh," Kate said with false charity, "I *know*. A lady ought not to mention a gentleman's wager. But then, you can hardly be deserving of the term *gentleman* if you've entered into that pact to seduce me."

That brought his shoulders straight up, and wiped all expression from his face. "Seduce you? But—"

"Am I making you uncomfortable?" Kate asked with pretend solicitousness. "Are you perhaps feeling as if your privacy has been violated by my inquiry? Now, perhaps, you can imagine how it feels for me to have my virtue discussed all over London."

"Actually—"

"Don't bother protesting. Tell the truth. Did you linger here, thinking you would have me in bed?"

"No!" he said in injured tones. Then he pressed his lips together, as if tasting something bitter. "To be perfectly truthful," he said in a subdued tone, "and come to think of it, *yes*, but—"

"My answer is 'no, thank you.' I already have everything a lady could wish for."

"Really?"

He was watching her intently now. She could imagine him reporting this speech to his friends. If he did, the sum of the gossip would be her words, not her clothing. Harcroft would hear, but he'd think nothing of it. Just another man, who failed to collect. Kate counted items off on her fingers. "I have a fulfilling life filled with charitable work. A doting father. Virtually unlimited pin money." She tapped her little finger and shot him another disarming smile. "Oh, yes. And my husband lives six thousand miles away. Now why in heaven's name do all you fools believe I should want to complicate my life with a messy, illicit love affair?"

He froze, then recovered himself enough to reach up and rub the tawny bristle on his chin. "Would you know," he said softly, "my solicitor was right. I should have shaved first."

"I assure you, your slovenly appearance makes not one iota of difference."

"It's not the beard." His hand clenched briefly into a fist at his side, and then relaxed.

She felt a grim delight at that sign of confusion. It wasn't fair to take all men to task for her husband's failings—but then, this one *had* set out to seduce her, and she was not in the mood to be kind. "You seem out of sorts," she said, imbuing her voice with a false charity. "And foolish. And bumbling. Are you quite sure you're not my errant husband?"

"Well, that's the thing." He glanced at her almost apologetically. And then he took another step towards her.

This close, she could see his chest expand on an inhale. He reached for her hand. She had time to pull away. She *ought* to pull away. His thumb and forefinger caught her wrist, as gently as if he were catching a dried leaf as it fell from a tree. His fingers found the precise spot where her glove ended and her flesh began. She might have been that leaf, ready to combust in one heated moment.

She desperately needed to escape, to reconstruct the feeling of success that had been so rudely taken from her. He smiled at her again, and his eyes twinkled ruefully. And suddenly, horribly, she knew what he was going to say. She knew why his eyes had seemed so unnaturally familiar.

She *did* know this man. She had imagined meeting him a thousand ways in the last three years. Sometimes, she had said nothing. Other times, she'd delivered cutting speeches. She always brought him to his knees, eventually, in apology, while she looked on regally.

There was nothing regal about her now. In all of her imaginings, not once had she met him wearing an ill-fitting servant's cloak, with smudges on her face.

Her fingers still burned where he touched her, and Kate jerked her hand away.

"You see," he said dryly, "I'm quite sure that I *am* your husband. And I'm not six thousand miles away any longer."

Unveiled

He was her bitterest enemy...

Ash Turner has waited a lifetime to seek revenge on the man who ruined his family—and at last the time for justice has arrived. At Parford Manor, he intends to take his place as the rightful heir to the dukedom, and settle an old score with the current duke once and for all. But when he arrives, he finds himself drawn to a tempting beauty who has the power to undo all his dreams of vengeance.

And her dearest love.

Lady Margaret knows she should despise the man who's stolen her fortune and her father's legacy—the man she's been ordered to spy on in the guise of a nurse. Yet the more she learns about the new duke, the less she can resist his smoldering appeal. Soon Margaret and Ash find themselves torn between old loyalties—and the tantalizing promise of passion.

Available February 1, 2011 from HQN Books
ISBN-10: 0373775431 ✳ISBN-13: 978-0373775439

Chapter One

SOMERSET, 1837

So this was how it felt to be a conquering hero.

Ash Turner—once plain Mr. Turner; now, so long as fate stayed Parliament's hand, the future Duke of Parford—sat back on his horse as he reached the crest of the hill.

The estate he would inherit was laid out in the valley before him. Stone walls hugged the curves of the limestone hill his horse stood on, breaking the brilliant apple-green of high summer into gentle, rolling squares of patchwork. A small cottage stood to the side of the road. He could hear the hushed whispers of the farm children, who had crept out to gawk at him as he passed.

Over the last few months, he'd become accustomed to getting gawked at.

Behind him, his younger brother's steed stamped and come to a halt. From this high vantage point, they could see Parford Manor—a massive four-story, five-winged affair, its brilliant windows glittering in the sunlight. Undoubtedly, someone had set a servant to watch for his arrival. Soon, the staff would spill out onto the front steps, arranging themselves in careful lines, ready to greet the man who would be their future master.

The man who'd stolen a dukedom.

A smile played over Ash's face. Once he inherited, nobody would gainsay him.

"You don't have to do this." The words came from behind him.

Nobody, that was, except his little brother.

Ash turned in the saddle. Mark was facing forward, looking at the manor below with an abstracted expression. That detached focus made him look simultaneously old, as if he deserved an elder's beard to go with that inexplicable wisdom, and at the same time, still unaccountably boyish.

"It's not right." Mark's voice was barely audible above the wind that whipped at Ash's collar.

Mark was seven years younger than Ash, which made him by most estimations barely an adult. But despite all that Mark had experienced, he had somehow managed to retain an aura of almost painful purity. He was the opposite of Ash—blond, where Ash's hair was dark; slim, where Ash's shoulders had broadened with years of labor. But most of all, Mark seemed profoundly, sacredly innocent, where Ash felt tired and profane. Perhaps that was why the last thing Ash wanted to do with his moment of victory was to dissect its ethics.

Instead, Ash shook his head. "You asked me to find you a quiet country home for these last weeks of summer, so you might work in peace." Ash spread his arms, palms up. "Well. Here you are."

Down in the valley, the first ranks of servants had begun to gather, jockeying for position on the wide steps leading up to the massive front doors.

Mark shrugged, as if this evidence of prosperity meant nothing to him. "A house back in Shepton Mallet would have done."

A tight knot formed in Ash's stomach. "You're not going back to Shepton Mallet. You're *never* going back there. Do you suppose I would simply kick you from a carriage at Market Cross and let you disappear for the summer?"

Mark finally broke his gaze from the tableau in front of them and met Ash's eyes. "Even by your extravagant standards, Ash, you must admit this is a bit much."

"You don't think I would make a good duke? Or you don't approve of the manner in which I inveigled a summer's invitation to the ducal manor?"

Mark simply shook his head. "I don't need this. *We* don't need this."

And therein lay Ash's problem. He wanted to make up for every last bit of his brothers' childhood deprivation. He wanted to repay every skipped meal in twelve-course dinners, gift a thousand pairs of gloves in exchange for every shoeless winter. He'd risked his life, building a fortune to ensure their happiness. And yet both his brothers declared themselves satisfied with a few prosaic simplicities.

But simplicities wouldn't make up for Ash's failure. So maybe he had overindulged when Mark finally asked him for a favor.

"Shepton Mallet would have been quiet," Mark said, almost wistfully.

"Shepton Mallet is halfway to dead." Ash clucked to his horse. As he did so, the wind stopped, and the sound echoed loudly. The horse started down the road towards the manor house.

Mark kicked his own mare into a trot and followed.

"You've never thought it through," Ash tossed over his shoulder. "With Richard and Edgar Dalrymple no longer able to inherit, you're fourth in line for a dukedom. There are a great many advantages to that. Opportunities will arise. Grab them with both hands. Life is meant to be lived, after all."

"Is that how you're describing your actions, this last six month? 'No longer able to inherit?'"

Ash ignored this sally. "You're young. You're handsome. I'm sure there are some very lovely milkmaids in Somerset who would be delighted to make the acquaintance of a man who is an arm's breadth from inheriting a dukedom."

Mark stopped his horse a few yards before the gate to the grounds. Ash felt a fillip of annoyance at the delay, but he halted, too.

"Say it," Mark said. "Say what you did to the Dalrymples. It's been nothing but one euphemism after another these last three months. If you can't even bring yourself to say it, you should never have done it."

"Christ. You're acting as if I killed them."

But Mark was looking at him, his blue eyes intense. In this mood, with the sun glancing off all that blonde hair, Ash wouldn't have been surprised if his brother had pulled a flaming sword from his saddlebag and proclaimed him barred from Eden forever. "Say it," Mark repeated.

And besides, his little brother so rarely asked anything of him. Ash would have given Mark whatever he wanted, so long as he just... well, *wanted*.

"Very well." He met his brother's eyes. "I brought the evidence of the Duke of Parford's first marriage before the ecclesiastical courts, and thus had his second marriage declared void for bigamy. The children resulting from that union were declared illegitimate and unable to inherit. Which left the Duke's long-hated fifth cousin, twice removed, as the presumptive heir. That would be me." Ash started his horse again. "I didn't do anything to the Dalrymples except tell the truth of what their own father had done all those years ago."

And he wasn't about to apologize for it, either.

Mark snorted and started his horse again. "And you didn't have to do that."

But he had. Ash didn't believe in foretellings or spiritual claptrap, but from time to time, he had... premonitions, perhaps, although that word smacked of the occult. A better phrase might have been that he possessed a sheer animal instinct. As if the reactive beast buried deep inside him could recognize truths that human senses, dulled by comfortable living, could not.

When he'd found about about Parford, he'd known with a blazing certainty: *If I become Parford, I can finally break my brothers free of the prison they've built for themselves.*

With that burden weighing down one side of the scales, no moral considerations could balance them to equipose. The disinherited Dalrymples meant nothing. Besides, after what Richard and Edmund had done to Mark? Really. He shed no tears for their loss.

The servants had finished gathering, and as Ash trotted up the drive, they held themselves at stiff attention. They were too well-trained to gawk, too polite to let more than a little rigidity infect their manner. Likely, they were too accustomed to their wages to do more than grouse about the upstart heir the courts had forced upon them.

They'd like him soon enough. Everyone always did.

"Who knows?" he said quietly. "Maybe one of these serving girls will catch your eye. You can have any one you'd like."

Mark favored him with an amused look. "Satan," he said, shaking his head, "get thee behind me."

Ash's steed came to a stop, and he dismounted slowly. The manor looked smaller than Ash remembered, the stone of its facade honey-golden, not bleak and imposing. It had shrunk from the unassailable fortress that had loomed in Ash's head all these decades. Now, it was just a house. A big house, yes, but not the dark menacing edifice he'd held in his memory.

The servants stood in painful, ordered rows. Ash glanced over them.

There were probably over a hundred gray-liveried retainers arrayed before him. He felt as sober as they appeared. Had there been the slightest danger of Mark accepting his cavalier offer, Ash would never have made it. These people were his dependents now—or they would be, once the current Duke passed away. His *duty*. Their prosperity would hang on his whim, as his had once hung on Parford's. It was a weighty responsibility.

I'm going to do better than that old bastard.

A vow, that, and one he meant every bit as much as the last promise he'd sworn, looking up at this building.

He was about to turn away to greet the major domo, who had stepped forward, when he saw her. She stood in the last row, high up the steps, her face almost obscured by the burly servant who stood before her. The wind started up again, as if the entire universe had been holding its breath up until this moment. She was looking directly at him, and Ash felt a cavernous hollow open up deep in his chest.

He'd never seen the woman before in his life. He couldn't have; he would have remembered the *feel* of her, the sheer rightness of it. She was pretty, even with that dark hair pulled into a severe knot and pinioned underneath a white lace cap, but it wasn't her looks that caught his attention. Ash had seen enough beautiful women in his time. Maybe it was her eyes, narrowed and steely, fixed on him as if he were the source of all that was wrong in the world. Maybe it was the set of her chin, so unyielding, so fiercely determined, when every face around hers mirrored uncertainty. Whatever it was, the sight of her struck him deep in his gut.

It reminded him of the cacophony of an orchestra as it tuned its instruments: dissonance, suddenly resolving into harmony. It was the rumble, not of thunder, but its low, rolling precursor, trembling on the horizon. It was all of that. It was none of that. It was sheer animal instinct, and it reached up and grabbed him by the throat. *Her. Her.*

Ash had never ignored his instincts before—not once. He swallowed hard as the major domo approached.

"One thing," he whispered to his brother. "The woman in the last row— third to the right? She's mine."

Before his brother could do more than frown at him, before Ash himself could do more than swallow the lingering feeling of sparks coursing through his veins, the major domo was upon them, bowing and introducing himself. Ash took a deep breath and focused on the man.

"Mr.—I mean, my—" The man paused, uncertain how to address Ash. With the Duke still alive, Ash, a mere distant cousin, held no title. And yet he had come here as heir to the dukedom, on the strictest orders from Chancery. Ash could guess at the careful calculation in the man's eyes: Should he risk offending the man who might well be his next master, or ought he adhere to the strict formalities required by etiquette?

Ash smiled. "Plain Mr. Turner will do. There's no need to worry about how you address me. I scarcely know what to call myself."

The man nodded and the taut muscles in his face relaxed. "Mr. Turner, shall I arrange a tour, or would you and your brother care to take some refreshment first?"

Ash's eyes wandered to the woman in the back row. She met his gaze, her eyes implacable, and a queer shiver ran down his spine. It was not lust itself he felt, but the premonition of desire, as if the wind that whipped around his cravat were whispering in his ears. *Her. Choose her.*

"Good luck," Mark muttered. "I don't believe she likes you all that much."

That much Ash had gleaned from the set of her jaw.

"No refreshment," Ash said aloud. "No rest. I want to know everything, and the sooner, the better. I'll need to speak with Parford as well. I'd best start as I mean to go on." He glanced back at the woman one last time, and then met his brother's eyes. "After all, I do enjoy a challenge."

Still Available

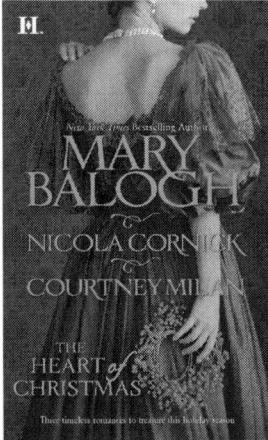

"This Wicked Gift,"
   in *The Heart of Christmas* Anthology
ISBN-10: 0373774273 ✻*ISBN-13: 978-0373774272*

Voted Best Romance Short Story of 2009,
   All About Romance
2010 RITA® Finalist, Best Novella category
Reader's Crown™ Finalist, Best Novella category

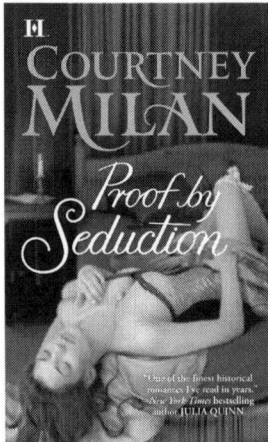

Proof by Seduction
ISBN-10: 0373774397 ✻ISBN-13: 9780373774395

"One of the finest historical romances I've read in
years. I am now officially a Courtney Milan fangirl."
   —Julia Quinn, #1 *New York Times* bestseller

Jennifer Haymore

Jennifer Haymore grew up on the Big Island of Hawaii, where she surfed, learned how to fly airplanes, raced bicycles, and developed a love for sailing. She was an avid reader and completely destroyed her eyesight by sneaking a flashlight under her covers and reading far into the nights — making her mother wonder why on earth she couldn't get up for school in the mornings...

Jennifer holds a bachelor's degree in Computer Science from UC Berkeley and a master's degree in Education from UCLA. Before she became a full-time writer she held various jobs from bookselling to teaching inner-city children to playing bit roles in soap operas.

You can find Jennifer in Southern California trying to talk her husband into yet another trip to England, helping her three children with homework while brainstorming a new five-minute dinner menu, or crouched in a corner of the local bookstore writing her next novel.

You can find out more about Jennifer by visiting http://www.jenniferhaymore.com.

Praise for Jennifer

"For jaded romance readers, Jennifer Haymore is an author to watch."
—Nicole Jordan, *New York Times* bestselling author

"Sweep-you-off-your-feet historical romance! Jennifer Haymore sparkles!"
—Liz Carlyle, *New York Times* bestselling author

"Haymore... perfectly blends a strong plot that twists like a serpent and has unforgettable characters to create a book readers will remember and re-read."
—*RT Book Reviews* magazine, 4½ stars, TOP Pick!

"Jennifer Haymore's books are sophisticated, deeply sensual, and emotionally complex."
—Elizabeth Hoyt, *New York Times* bestselling author

A Touch of Scandal

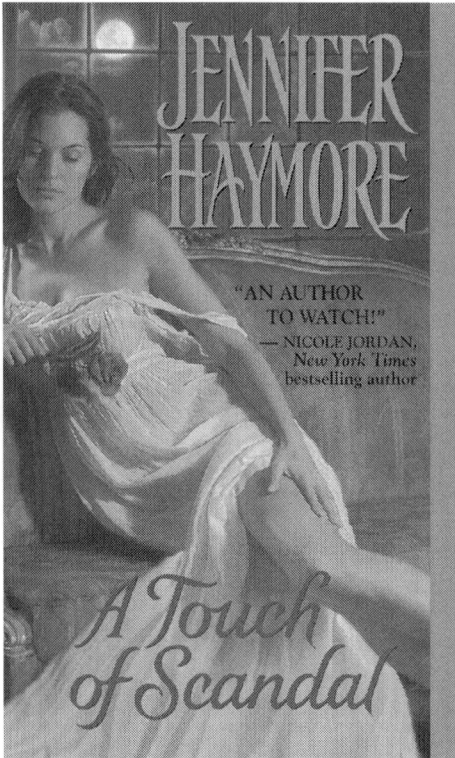

"AN AUTHOR
TO WATCH!"
— NICOLE JORDAN,
New York Times
bestselling author

The last thing Garrett, Duke of Calton, expects to find while tracking his sworn enemy is the delectable, mysterious Kate. This beautiful servant girl rouses a longing the battle-scarred ex-soldier had never hoped to feel again. But when she turns out to be the sister of the man he seeks, he's convinced he's been betrayed.

Kate knows her duty to her family, yet how can she ignore Garrett's powerful pull on her heart? Or the heady temptation of his stolen-and sizzling-kisses? Scandal has followed the duke since the war. Now the greatest shock of all is on its way— the one that can separate Garrett and Kate forever.

Available April 1, 2010, from Forever
ISBN-10: 0446540277 ✳ISBN-13: 978-0446540278

Chapter One

A bothersome heat crept into Kate's cheeks as she hurried through the narrow, dimly lit passageway. If only she could learn how to hide her thoughts.

Taking a deep breath, she forcefully slowed her step, squared her shoulders, and lowered her eyes. She was simply a servant, finished with her duties for the day, ready to take the three-mile walk home. Not a flustered woman rushing out to a secret secluded spot to watch a strange man—no, a *god*, more like—bathe in the nude.

Kate paused at the threshold of the parlor. "Pardon me, my lady?"

She bobbed a curtsy as her mistress looked up from the novel she was reading. Lady Rebecca always kept her head firmly tucked in a book. A pang of sympathy shot into Kate's heart when the younger woman's haunted blue eyes met hers.

"Yes?" Lady Rebecca lowered the thick volume to her lap.

Lady Rebecca was the sister of a duke, and her breeding showed in her expression, in her bearing, and in her mannerisms. Today she wore a plain white muslin gown with a gauze fichu tucked into its rounded neckline, but neither the simplicity of her dress nor her relaxed position on the sofa diminished the evidence of her nobility. She'd kicked her shoes off and settled on the plum-colored velvet with her legs tucked beneath her. With her slender build, her coal black hair, and her midnight blue eyes, Lady Rebecca was one of the most beautiful women Kate had ever laid eyes on, but there was a sweetness about her, a vulnerability, that drew Kate, that made her want to protect her, even to share secrets.

No, Kate reprimanded herself. A shiver skittered down her spine. Some secrets were best left unspoken. *Forever.*

Had circumstances been different, she and Lady Rebecca might have been friends. *Sisters.* But Kate was merely a servant, albeit an unconventional one, given that she slept apart from the rest of the household. Still, she wished she had the freedom to sit beside Lady Rebecca and engage in a lively discussion about whatever it was she read with such passion.

"What is it, Kate?" Lady Rebecca gazed at her without really seeing her, but Kate was accustomed to it. It was how aristocrats always looked at her—as an object rather than a human. She couldn't blame them, for they didn't know any better. It infuriated Mama, though.

"Might I be dismissed, ma'am? I've prepared your bed, brought up fresh water, and set out your nightclothes for Annie." Kate's smile wobbled. The knowledge that she might see *him* again had butterfly wings tickling her insides. She fought not to squirm, but the mere thought of the handsome stranger made her skin prickle.

Lady Rebecca frowned. "Is it your little brother? Is he very unwell?"

The lady knew Reggie was the sole reason Kate walked home every night. Her younger brother was a sickly boy, and while Mama cared for him well enough during the day, she didn't like her sleep interrupted, so Kate was there for him through the long, sometimes difficult nights.

"Well . . ." Kate was a horrible liar, but she needn't exaggerate in order to answer the question. It also wasn't necessary to explain that her reasons for wanting to leave early today had nothing to do with Reggie's health. "He has been coughing quite a lot."

"Oh, the poor thing." Lady Rebecca waved her hand. "Of course, Kate. Please do go—I know you've a distance to walk, and—" she squinted at the drab chintz curtain covering the single square window, "—it's near dark isn't it?"

"I think so." *Oh, please, Lord, let him be there today. Let me not be too late.*

"Yes, well . . ." Lady Rebecca glanced across the room at the door that led downstairs. The hope in her eyes was unmistakable. "The master should be home soon."

Kate nodded. Her elder brother, William, was Lady Rebecca's husband, and he liked Kate to be gone before he arrived. He found it awkward to be with his sister and wife in the same room, and he feared Kate would betray them both. Kate didn't blame him. First of all, it was horribly awkward to her as well. Second, deception was not her forte. From the beginning, she'd felt the worst part of this whole arrangement was the duplicity inherent in it. She understood why it must be, but it still twisted her stomach.

Lady Rebecca turned back to Kate. "Of course you may go."

"Thank you, ma'am. I'll be here when you wake in the morning." Kate dipped into another curtsy and tried not to break into a run as she crossed the room to the opposite door. Even so, the clack of her shoe heels on the wood floor announced her hasty departure, and from the corner of her eye, she saw Lady Rebecca's brow tilt in bemusement as she watched her go.

The cottage was elegant and expensive, but certainly neither as elegant nor as expensive as a duke's sister was accustomed to. Willy was in financial straits and only employed four servants—Kate, the cook, the maid-of-all-work, and the manservant, John. The other female servants lived in the small room in the attic and John slept in a loft above the stable, but Kate walked back and forth to her home at Debussey Manor daily.

It was far less help than someone of Lady Rebecca's breeding expected. Yet she never complained. Kate admired her for that.

Her cheeks flaming despite all her efforts to douse the fire in them, Kate descended the last step and emerged into the drawing room. Glancing up, she stopped in her tracks, stiffening. John lay on the tasseled chaise longue, his stockinged feet crossed atop the cream-colored silk and his arm flung over his forehead.

He cracked one lid open to gaze at her with a green eye, and Kate pursed her lips in distaste.

"Leaving?" he asked.

"Yes," she answered curtly. Untying her apron, she spun round and strode to the closet behind the stairwell.

Feeling John's reptilian eye on her, she pulled off her apron and cap, hung them, and after a moment of consideration, decided to leave her cloak here overnight. It had been a warm day, so surely it wouldn't be too cold to walk without it in the morning, and it would be a nuisance to carry both ways.

"You look pretty today, kitty. That color becomes you."

She cast a look down at her dull pale brown work dress. How pleasant to know that brown was her color. "Thank you," she pushed out.

He chuckled but Kate didn't look in his direction. John was negligent, arrogant, lazy, and, with his greased hair and pointed beak nose, unappealing. Whenever Willy was near, John's manner was obsequious to the point of inducing nausea, but when Willy wasn't home, he strutted about the place as if he owned it, even going so far as to be disrespectful to Lady Rebecca. Nothing raised Kate's ire more than to see that man's disdainful behavior toward her mistress.

She turned from the closet and strode to the front door. Opening it, she stepped into the pleasant late-summer evening. As she closed the door, John's voice drifted lazily out. "Tomorrow, then, pretty kitty."

Her lips twisted, and when the door met its frame, she shoved it hard. The tiny slam brought her a small measure of satisfaction.

If John thought to seduce her with false flattery, he ought to think again. No man had seduced her yet, though a few had tried. She'd promised herself long ago to never go down that particular perilous road. And with a man like John . . . not a chance.

Still, it was best to stay away from him and make certain to avoid being alone with him. He didn't strike her as the kind of man who'd take her rejection to heart.

Kate paused on the tiny landing and took a deep breath. Was she a hypocrite? She shook her head, thinking not. *Watching* was a wholly different action from *doing*, after all. And John the skinny, lazy manservant was a wholly different creature from the bronze god at the pool.

Kenilworth's gently curving High Street was deserted for the moment. The setting sun cast an orange glow across the rooftops, and the houses and shops abutting the road shimmered in the haze.

She turned and strode down the street with purpose, her shoes scraping against the hard-packed dirt. Ahead, the shoemaker's widow, dressed in black with a dark shawl draped over her shoulders, emerged from one of the pretty neighboring cottages. Kate bobbed and murmured a polite greeting when they passed each other. The woman wished her a good evening as the clatter of wheels and the sound of hooves heralded a coach and four coming from behind. Kate glanced over her shoulder to see the carriage, a closed, lacquered black beast, approaching, tossing up a billow of dirt in its wake.

She picked up her skirts and hurried across the street in front of it, slipping through a broken slat in the old wooden gate and stepping onto a narrow path in the field beyond just in time to avoid a choking spray of dust. Through the gold-tinged trees loomed the tall, jagged, ivy-covered ruins of Kenilworth Castle. Keeping the castle to her right, Kate followed the overgrown trail that led along the bank of the brook. She skirted fallen branches and dead leaves, and before long grime caked her shoes and dampness seeped through her stockings.

Her heart thudded with a dull cadence, heavy in her chest. Under the coarse wool of her dress, her skin flushed with excitement. Would he be there today? He wasn't yesterday, but she'd seen him four times in the past week, swimming in the small lake created by the ruin of a dam that had once formed the castle moat.

The air grew warm and close. Branches cracked under her feet, and leaves rustled. The faint drone of insects hummed in the air as twilight approached. She'd taken the long way, and it'd be full dark by the time she arrived home, but she cared about that just about as much as she cared about her wet feet and mud-soaked hem. Not a whit.

She slowed as the creek turned northward, and with her lower lip trapped between her teeth, she concentrated on placing her footfalls so her steps would be quiet.

A splash sounded in the distance, and Kate halted and looked up. Beyond a thick copse of greenery just ahead, the pool glimmered in the gathering dusk, its surface rippling.

Someone had just dived in. *He* had just dived in.

Kate swallowed hard and crept forward, crouching so he wouldn't see her behind the clusters of brambles and bushes. She ducked behind a particularly dense bush at the water's edge and peeked around it.

Just as the waves on the pool's surface began to settle, he emerged from the depths with his back to her. He rose until the water lapped eagerly at his narrow waist. For the tiniest fraction of a second, she wished she could be that water.

His thick shoulder rippled with muscle as he reached up to thrust a hand through his glistening blond hair.

Surely this man couldn't be human. He was perfectly built—like one of the gods she'd learned about when she spied on Mama reading to her brothers. Tall, muscular, his skin bronzed from the sun, as hard and beautiful and intimidating as Apollo himself. He shook his head, sending blond shoulder-length curls flying and a cascade of golden drops showering into the water. Then he dove again, his taut—and quite shockingly bare—backside emerging from the water before his entire body disappeared beneath the surface.

A pleasurable shudder coursed through Kate, leaving a low burn to simmer deep inside her.

The god-man swam like a fish. Perhaps he wasn't Apollo at all, though he rather looked like she'd always imagined Apollo. Perhaps he was Poseidon—a young, clean-shaven Poseidon. Perhaps this time when he emerged, he'd be carrying his golden trident. She held her breath, waiting, frozen.

Kate had been born at Kenilworth and raised at Debussey Manor, and she knew without a doubt this man didn't hail from these parts. What was he doing here? And why did he come here—this place that had been her secret spot for so many years—to bathe? The sight of him, and his very strong, very *naked* body, was so far removed from her realm of reality that it didn't seem all too farfetched to think that a lightning bolt had deposited him straight from Olympus.

He rose from the water again, this time farther away but facing her. She stared in fascination at the jagged scar near his waist, and when her gaze traveled up his solid torso and over his rugged face, she saw the second scar, a terrible knot glaring red just above his left eyebrow.

The imperfections on his otherwise perfect form emphasized the fact that this was not a god, but a very human man indeed. A man who'd seen, experienced, and ultimately survived terrible things.

He rubbed the water out of his eyes and opened them. His sky blue gaze settled directly on her.

She jerked her head behind the bush, gulping back a gasp. Her heart thundered in her ears. A bead of sweat trickled down the side of her face. Controlling her breaths, she froze in her crouched position and squeezed her eyes shut. She couldn't move, because now he'd surely hear her. Her best option was to remain still and quiet, keep herself hidden behind the bush, and pray he hadn't seen her.

She should fear this giant, intimidating man, but that wasn't why she prayed he hadn't seen her. No, she prayed he hadn't seen her because if he had, she wouldn't be able to watch his sculpted nude body anymore.

She let out a long, silent sigh through pursed lips. It was the undeniable truth. As much as she'd fought against it, she was hopelessly and thoroughly debauched. If not in body, at least in thought. The man could be a murderer or a lunatic, and all she cared about was spying on him.

Not only was she debauched, she was an idiot.

Perhaps he hadn't seen her. He had just opened his eyes after being submerged in water, and surely it would take a second or two for him to focus on an object as far away as her. And with her brown hair and brown dress, she blended into the landscape like a chameleon.

She'd remain hidden for a few moments longer, then make a hasty, as-quiet-as-possible retreat.

Keeping her eyes closed, she hugged her knees to her chest and counted to a hundred. All was silent for a while, but when she reached sixty, she heard splashing from the direction of the pond. Clearly he'd resumed his sport.

Ninety-nine. One hundred.

She released a relieved breath and raised her lids.

And found herself gazing into his rugged face.

She blinked several times in disbelief, trying to clear her vision as he stared at her with narrowed blue eyes from his position on his haunches an arm's length away. A frown creased his handsome features. Rivulets of water streamed from his golden hair and plastered a loose white shirt to his broad, imposing shoulders.

He'd been watching her. Spying on her in silence—probably throwing rocks into the water to mislead her.

With a squeal of fright, Kate stumbled to her feet. Her legs caught in her skirts, but she kicked them free. Brambles clawed at her dress, ripping the fabric as she lunged away.

She'd gone no farther than two steps when he clapped an arm around her waist and yanked her back. She stumbled and would have fallen had his hard body not ensnared her like a net.

Kate trembled all over. Small, pathetic whimpers bubbled from her throat as she futilely tried to twist away.

His warm, damp torso pressed against her back. He smelled fresh and clean, like hay drying in the sunlight, with an underlying almond scent she instinctually recognized as purely his.

His arm crossed over the front of her chest, pinning her against him. The lock of his embrace rendered her utterly helpless.

"Who are you?" he demanded. He bent his head, and the trace of beard on his jaw scraped against the shell of her ear. "And why are you watching me?"

His voice, low and rough, stroked over her body like a coarse towel, causing every inch of Kate's skin to explode into flame.

Panic wouldn't help her now. She must stave it off, be as brave as a knight battling a rampaging dragon. For several moments, trapped in the steel of the stranger's arms, she worked to control her gasping breaths and to stop her limbs from shaking like autumn leaves in a gale.

Finally, she sucked in a lungful of air. Staring straight over the pool, now glowing purple in the twilight, she said, "My name is Katherine, sir. I'm very glad to meet you. Lovely evening, isn't it?"

A Season of Seduction

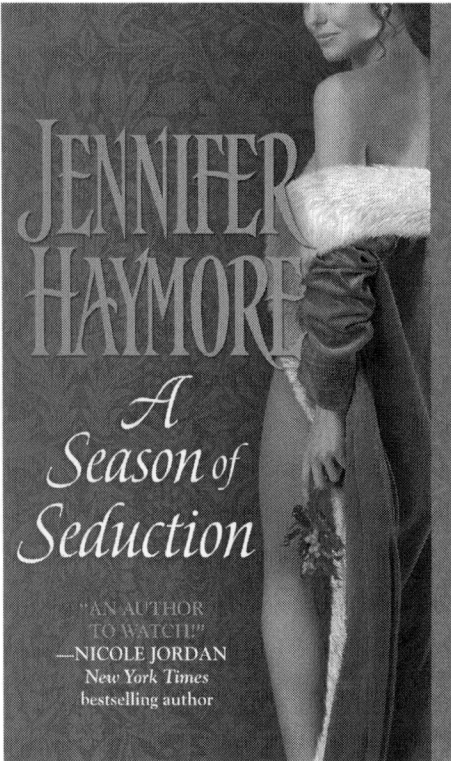

Although the widowed Lady Rebecca has sworn off marriage, men are another matter. London's cold winter nights have her dreaming of warmer pursuits-like finding a lover to satisfy her hungry heart. Someone handsome, discreet, and most importantly as uninterested in marriage as she is. Someone like Jack Fulton.

A known adventurer and playboy, Jack seems like the perfect choice. There's just one problem: Jack isn't interested in an affair. He needs the beautiful, mysterious Lady Rebecca to be his wife. And he doesn't have much time to persuade her. A secret from Jack's past is about to surface, and by Christmas Day he'll be either married to Rebecca or swaying from the hangman's noose...

JENNIFER HAYMORE

A Season *of* Seduction

"AN AUTHOR TO WATCH!"
—NICOLE JORDAN
New York Times
bestselling author

Available September 28, 2010, from Forever
ISBN-10: 0446540285 ✳ISBN-13: 978-0446540285

Chapter One

Tonight I will be his.

Becky closed her eyes as her maid, Josie, sprinkled rosewater on her hair, and a shudder spiraled up her spine. *Jack Fulton.* The dashing sailor who'd recently returned to London after many years at sea. Tonight would be the first time she'd touched a man intimately in four years. Tonight, she would give herself to him, wholly and completely.

She'd been acquainted with Jack for a month now, but she knew little of his true nature, and he knew little of hers. When they were together, they conversed easily about the past and the present, but they lived in the moment and never dug beyond the surface.

She preferred it that way. Nevertheless, there was something about him that made her yearn to burrow beyond his hardened shell and discover what lay beneath that rugged, handsome surface.

She shook herself a little to toss away the thought. Josie's round face scrunched in disapproval as a tendril of hair dislodged from Becky's coiffure, and the maid gave a long-suffering sigh before she went back to smoothing her mistress's hair.

Becky opened her eyes and stared into her friend Cecelia's dressing room mirror. It was hypocritical of her to want to learn more about Jack Fulton. She certainly didn't want him delving into her soul. She'd locked herself up tight long ago and never intended to reveal herself again. Not even to a lover. As long as she kept her heart safely guarded, tonight would set her free. Jack couldn't hurt her—she wouldn't allow that to happen. He *could*, however, release her from the lonely prison that had held her captive for years. He could make her feel alive again.

"You're thinking about something, Becky. I see it in your face."

Becky's met her friend's gaze in the mirror. Cecelia, Lady Devore clasped her hands behind her back. She stood in the center of the room, one of her guest bedchambers. Her white satin dress with its high collar and broad belt of embroidered crimson emphasized the slightness of her build, and the sweep of her chocolate-colored hair accentuated her elegant swan's neck and pointed chin.

Earlier this evening, Cecelia had fetched Becky from her brother's house on the pretense of taking her to the opera. But there would be no opera for Becky tonight. Instead, Cecelia would deposit Becky at a respectable hotel where she intended to have a not-so-respectable tryst with a seafaring rogue who possessed a hint of the gentleman. Or was it that he was a gentleman with a hint of the rogue?

There was no denying that Jack Fulton came from respectable stock—his father was one of the king's privy councilors, his eldest brother possessed parliamentary ambitions, and his middle brother was a captain in His Majesty's Navy. Jack wasn't at the pinnacle of the aristocracy, like Becky's family or even Cecelia's, but his bloodlines were quite dignified, indeed.

One look at him, though, and anyone could detect that there was something enticingly disreputable about him. An air of danger—of roguishness—that made Becky's pulse flutter and her limbs turn to mush. His looks appealed to her in a startling way. She was more familiar with the sleek, pale, soft bucks of the London ton, but Jack was suntanned, with a permanent crease between his eyebrows and lines fanning from the edges of his eyes that deepened when he smiled. His hair and sideburns were trimmed short, and were a color of brown just a shade lighter than his eyes. His lips were light pink, and they had a wicked curve to them that matched the glint in his eyes. Together, those eyes and lips had featured in her erotic dreams for the past month.

Cecelia cleared her throat softly, jerking Becky from those scandalous thoughts.

"Yes…" Becky admitted slowly. "I *am* thinking about something."

Cecelia's dark eyes gleamed with understanding. Still, she wanted Becky to voice it. "Tell."

Becky glanced at her maid and dismissed her with a small movement of her hand. In complete silence but with a mulish pucker to her mouth, Josie corked the bottle of rosewater, set it on the table, curtsied, and went away.

When the door clicked shut, Becky said, "I think tonight is the night."

"Do you?" Cecelia's voice was soft. Satin rustled as she glided over the carpet, closer to the dressing table. "You've grown fond of our Mr. Fulton, haven't you?"

Resting her crooked arm on the shining oak surface of the dressing table, Becky wiggled her fingers. The last two fingers on her left hand tingled often, but she'd learned to take comfort from the sensation. The tingling was a part of her, like her bent, badly healed arm. It reminded her of a time in her life she'd do well not to forget.

"It's not that I've grown fond of him, per se. I've grown fond of…parts of him."

"Ah." Cecelia's lips tilted with mischief. "Parts you wish to become more intimately acquainted with."

Becky's cheeks heated, and she shifted uncomfortably in the chair. "Well, yes, I suppose you could put it that way."

Cecelia's renowned bluntness extended to matters most people kept to themselves. This was one attribute of her friend that had originally drawn Becky when they'd met during the Season earlier this year. She found Cecelia's matter-of-fact approach to mankind's baser nature both refreshing and shocking.

When London society had left en masse after the Season ended, Becky's family had remained. Cecelia had stayed in London, too, citing an utter loathing of country life. With most of society gone, Cecelia and Becky had turned to each other for company almost daily. Even now, however, despite their months of friendship, Becky still blushed often in the other woman's presence.

Cecelia's brow smoothed, and her lips softened into an expression of compassion. She laid an elegant, long-fingered hand on Becky's shoulder. "I am pleased for you. It has been so long."

Four years had passed since Becky had last lain with a man. She'd been so eager with her husband—eager to learn and eager to please. She had reveled in every touch they'd shared. Until things had turned sour.

"Too long," Cecelia added.

Becky blew out a breath and gave her friend an exasperated look. "Indeed, you are quite spoiled, Cecelia. Most widows never touch another man after their husbands die."

Cecelia, whose natural demeanor was one of haughty aristocracy, managed to appear even haughtier. Her thin, dark eyebrows arched into peaks. "Well, that is their loss. I lost my husband the same year you lost yours, and as you know, many men have warmed my bed since." She shrugged. "I shall offer no apologies for it. I love men."

Becky twisted her lips. "Really? I wouldn't say so. As a whole, I'd say you take a rather cynical approach to the male sex."

Cecelia laughed lightly and patted Becky's shoulder. "Of course you are right. I daresay men are most appealing when they're in my bed naked and occupying their mouths with pursuits other than talking."

Tiny hairs danced on end at the back of Becky's neck, and she wrenched her gaze away from her friend. When they'd last met, Jack had kissed her. The erotic touch of his lips had sent electric bolts shooting through her body, reminding her that no matter how long she kept it confined, her innate passion would never disappear.

"You're ready, Becky." Cecelia gave her shoulder an encouraging squeeze.

"I'm not certain."

"I know it is what you want. And I know that whatever should happen between you and Mr. Fulton tonight, you're well equipped for it."

In the past few months, Cecelia had drawn Becky outside the tight confines of her loving but protective family. Late one night after a few glasses of claret, Becky confessed her secret desires to her friend, and Cecelia had taken it upon herself to candidly teach her all about how a widow should properly manage an affair—from the seduction to the culmination to what must take place afterward.

She was as ready as she'd ever be.

"I feel so heartless." Staring into the mirror at Cecelia, she ran a fingertip along the smooth neckline of her white muslin overdress. She'd worn a heavy silk opera dress to Cecelia's house, but that dress now hung in the oak paneled wardrobe across from the dressing table. She intended to remove the overdress before she went to him tonight. The translucent gown underneath would make her intentions clear. "Somehow it feels wrong—immoral—to approach such intimate topics so carelessly."

Cecelia shook her head firmly and clasped her hands behind her back. "You mustn't feel that way. I believe this is one of the weaknesses of our sex—we become so overwrought in matters of carnal love that we are unable to see them for what they are."

Becky frowned up at her friend in the mirror. "And what are they?"

"Simple fleshly pursuits. Completely separate from matters of the heart."

"Surely there must be an overlap between matters of the flesh and matters of the heart."

"Sometimes there is," Cecelia admitted. "But that is generally not the case. It is a rare specimen of a man who allows his carnal desires to trickle under his skin in such a manner." Smiling, she waved her hand. "Yes, yes, I know your brother is one of them. But one need only survey the men of our class to prove my hypothesis."

Becky returned her friend's smile, then rose from the dressing table. She was ready. Trustworthy Josie, despite her impertinence, remained ever tight-lipped about her mistress's affairs and would remain here until Becky returned in the morning. Cecelia would accompany her to the hotel, leave her to her privacy with Jack, and return for her at two o'clock.

"No doubt you are right." Becky straightened her spine. "Never fear, Cecelia, I will remember everything you have taught me. My heart will remain uninvolved. Whatever becomes of the time I spend with Mr. Fulton, I shall possess fond memories of all that we will share."

Cecelia took her hand and squeezed it, smiling at her.

Becky hoped she was telling the truth. She *wanted* to be telling the truth. Yet she was terrified, for though she would try with all her might to heed her friend's warnings, she feared Jack Fulton had already melted away a piece of her armor and had begun to burrow beneath it.

Drawing on the gloves the butler had just handed him, Jack glanced at the Earl of Stratford. "Everything in place?"

Stratford nodded, then cocked a blond brow. "I feel it imperative to ask you one final time: Are you certain about this course? I am not personally acquainted with the woman, but her family is formidable. If they were to discover that you planned it—"

Jack raised his hand. "Easy, man. No one else knows. No one will ever know."

Stratford was the only man in London he trusted with his plan. Jack had returned three months ago after a twelve-year absence from England to discover most of his childhood acquaintances had matured into weak, foppish creatures. He'd met the earl one night at a tavern on the Strand and discovered he was neither.

In the past weeks, Jack had learned a little of the man's past. Like Jack, the earl had suffered a great loss. That experience had done much to form the man he was today. He was well-known as a profligate rake, immoral and debauched.

He was the kind of man the mamas of the *ton* cautioned their innocent daughters against.

Despite the abundant warnings against him, however, with his devil-may-care indifference, his stylish good looks, his sandy blond hair several shades lighter than Jack's, and his pugilist's build, Stratford managed to lure every female that came within his proximity. The earl managed his reputation with a devilish glint in his blue eyes and a carefree smile. If Jack hadn't been accustomed to such feelings himself, he never would have recognized the bone-deep misery and weariness within his friend.

The two men walked through the front door of the earl's townhouse and into St. James's Square. The sun streamed through a thick haze, and leaves and rubbish tumbled down the street, propelled by a stiff breeze. The wind had whipped away the sooty smells of the city, leaving the crisp scent of the late autumn air in its wake.

Staring over the windswept square, Jack tugged at the black woolen lapels of his coat, pulling it more tightly about him. Two carriages rattled past, followed by several men on horseback and a milk cart. He glanced at his friend, who had paused at the top of the stairs to button his stylish dark gray topcoat.

"I need this," he said, just loudly enough for the earl to hear over the sounds of the street.

Stratford paused, his hand on the stair rail. An amethyst ring winked at Jack from the earl's fourth finger. "I know."

Jack spoke flatly. "It is the only way. I haven't much time. I'll not run from England with my tail between my legs."

"Of course." Stratford's tone was mild, but he gazed at him from beneath the brim of his hat, his blue eyes probing. "I'd choose a different course. But I am not you."

"No," Jack agreed, his voice tight. "You are not."

The earl shuddered, the stiffness in his shoulders evaporated, and he descended the remaining two steps with easy grace. "I possess no desire to be shackled to anyone. Ever."

Neither had Jack. Not until he'd seen Lady Rebecca—*Becky*. He'd first glimpsed her six weeks ago at the British Museum. He'd followed her at a distance, observed how she'd clutched her arm to her chest as she studied the artifacts in studious silence while her companions gossiped and chatted amongst themselves. A part of him had softened. Standing apart from the others, she looked fragile and distant. She was beautiful, delicate, seraphic. But something about her, some dark edge he couldn't quite place his finger on, reminded him of himself.

In the ensuing days, he'd learned she was the widowed sister of the eccentric Duke of Calton. At the tender age of eighteen, she'd lost her husband and then she'd injured her arm badly in a carriage accident, which explained the way she'd guarded it so carefully at the museum. Though four years had passed since the accident and death of her husband, her family reputedly hovered over her and protected her virtue as though she were a virgin debutante.

As Jack learned more about her, understanding dawned. She was the answer to his dilemma.

He'd discovered that Cecelia, Lady Devore, was a bosom friend of his target. Fortunately for him, the lady had been one of Stratford's conquests, and they remained on civil terms. Stratford had arranged an introduction, and upon meeting Jack and hearing of his interest in Lady Rebecca firsthand, Lady Devore's cool, cunning gaze had swept over him, and she'd agreed to discuss the prospect of presenting him to Lady Rebecca.

The next day Lady Devore sent a note naming a date, time, and place—a room in a small, elegant but unassuming hotel near the Strand.

He'd seen Lady Rebecca five times. Lady Devore had chaperoned the first meeting, but they'd met alone since. They'd dined, they'd played chess, they'd talked late into the night. She had played the pianoforte for him while he'd watched raptly, his body hardening at the way her teeth grazed over her lower lip as she focused on the notes.

He was tired of being teased. He was tired of shaving through her layers of shyness. He knew she wanted him—he witnessed it when her eyes followed him across a room, when her breath caught as his fingertips grazed her cheek. He'd kissed her two nights ago, and she'd responded with breathless passion.

She was ready.

More importantly, he was running out of time. He would be married—or dead—before Christmas.

Tonight would seal their future.

Tonight would be the first night of the rest of his life with Lady Rebecca Fisk.

Still Available from Jennifer Haymore...

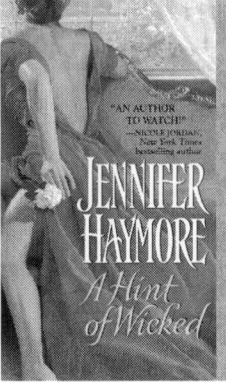

A Hint of Wicked
ISBN-10: 0446540293 ✳ ISBN-13: 978-0446540292

"A Hint of Wicked is amazing... one of the best historical romances I have read this year."
    —Fallen Angel Reviews

...and writing as Dawn Halliday

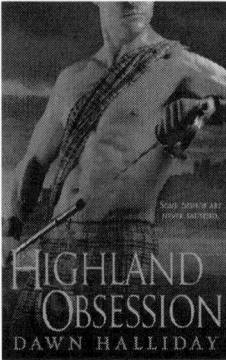

Highland Obsession
ISBN-10: 0451227018 ✳ ISBN-13: 978-0451227010

"Highland Obsession is on fire—a scorching page turner from cover to cover!"
    —Monica McCarty, New York Times bestseller

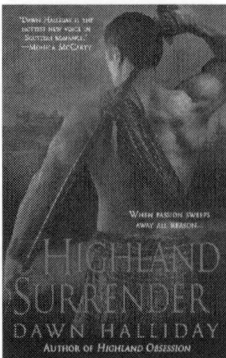

Highland Surrender
ISBN-10: 045122924X ✳ ISBN-13: 978-0451229243

"A delightfully sexy love story."
    —RT Book Reviews magazine

Tiffany Clare

Deciding that life had far more to offer than a nine to five job, bickering children in the evening and housework of any kind, Tiffany Clare opened up her laptop to rediscover her love of the written word. Tiffany writes historical romances set in the Victorian era. She lives in Toronto with her ever-patient photographer husband, two mischievous children and one hyperactive cat.

You can find out more about Tiffany by visiting her website at http://www.tiffanyclare.com.

Praise for Tiffany

"Tiffany Clare writes a swoon-worthy romance filled with rich details and vivid characters. Any readers wishing for a bold and sweeping historical romance need look no further—Tiffany Clare is a treasure of an author!"
    —Lisa Kleypas, *New York Times* bestselling author

"Exotic, bold, and captivating. Tiffany Clare's rich, sensual prose is delightful indulgence!"
    —Alexandra Hawkins, author of *Till Dawn with the Devil*

"Dazzling, daring, and different! *The Surrender of a Lady* will have you turning the pages until you finish, no matter how late it gets. Tiffany Clare is a brilliant new talent in historical romance."
    —Anna Campbell, award winning and RITA® nominated author

The Surrender of a Lady

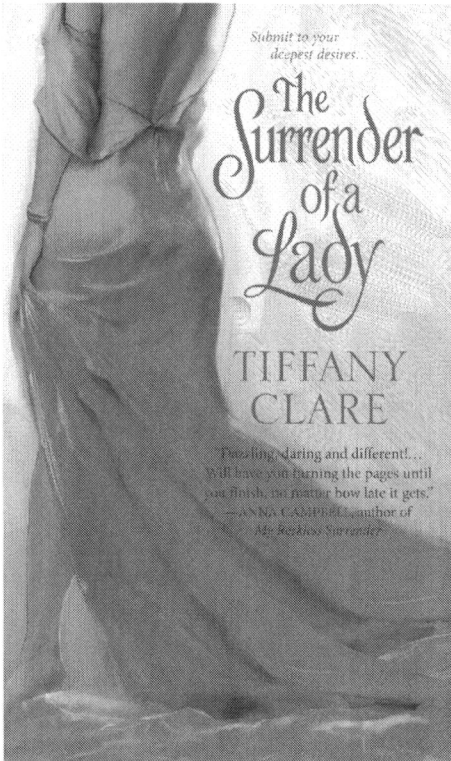

Submit to your deepest desires...

In the first of a stunning new series, a young English lady is thrust into the decadent life of a harem—and into the arms of the man she has never been able to forget...

The price of passion...

Sold. With one word, Lady Elena Ravenscliffe's destiny changes forever. Forced into Constantinople's slave market to pay off her late husband's debts and save her son, Elena reinvents herself as Jinan—a harem girl adored by the rich lords who bid on her favors. But one man instantly sees through her façade.

...is complete surrender.

Griffin Summerfield, Marquess of Rothburn, let Elena slip through his fingers years ago. When he recognizes her on the auction block, he pays an outrageous sum to possess her even if it is for a short period of time. But when his deadline looms, Griffin will risk all in a desperate bid to make her his—and his alone...

Available September 28, 2010, from St. Martin's Paperbacks
ISBN-10: 0312372116 ✳ISBN-13: 978-0312372118

Chapter One
Slave Trader

"What do you mean, you'll work this out? You've gambled me away! I'm your wife, for heaven's sake!"

"Elena, please. Calm yourself. I'll think of something."

Did he really think to placate her after such a proclamation? She was entitled to more than a fit of rage right now. She was livid. "It's a little late for alternatives."

With her hand clutched over her chest, Elena felt the frantic beating of her heart beneath her thin nightgown. She was desperate to calm it and her nerves; otherwise she'd never think this through rationally. What he said couldn't be true. It was outrageous and too despicable to contemplate. A sickening sense of fear had her itching to crawl through the floor.

Two eunuchs flanked her husband. One was pure ebony, with a wide, firm frame common to the palace eunuchs, and had a severe, menacing posture that terrified the wits out of her. The bitter fear made her want to retreat to the other side of the room. Out of his reach. The other was shorter and fatter, with a round, pockmarked face and a red sash about his waist that accentuated his girth. Whenever he spoke to her husband, she caught a glimpse of gold teeth behind his anger-thinned lips. The sight made her quiver in disgust.

Both projected an air of command. They wore traditional caftans, and their forearms bore large gold cuffs, their fists were loose at their sides. One couldn't mistake their intent. Nor did their poised outward appearance fool her; they would not be stopped from collecting payment. It was just a matter of sorting out *what* that payment was.

"Tell them to leave, Robert. We will think of something." They would leave Constantinople to escape what her husband had done. Start afresh, just as they'd done last year. This place was supposed to have been their refuge. A place where their son could grow up without being looked down upon by society because of his father's recklessness.

Foolish of her to think Robert had changed. He never did the decent thing by his family. How had she been duped into believing he'd mend his bad habits after all these years?

"I'm afraid it's not so easy as that."

She knew he played at being calm with those men hovering around. They were almost enough to frighten her into silence. But she knew her husband wouldn't defend her, he never had. Not from the first moment he'd set his sights on her.

She swallowed back the fear closing in around her and stilled her shaking hands by clasping them together. She needed to remain strong, to remember that Robert was a betraying swine. If she focused on that thought, she might be able to talk her way out of this.

She would not be the bargaining chip for his gambling debts.

Tilting her chin up, she looked down her nose at her husband. "I refuse to go."

Yet she knew in her heart that payment had been made in the form of one young, nubile wife, not yet six months from the birthing bed. She began to believe these men wouldn't leave without her, but what did they plan to do with her, a woman still showing the signs of childbearing? Did they fancy such sport as she? She was no pale-skinned odalisque.

There had to be a solution, something to stall them. She just didn't know what would work.

The back of her knees hit the worn damask settee. She sat with a thump, fingers worrying a small tear on the edge of the seat. If one looked around the room it was more than obvious money was not abundant in this household. The floral printed paper on the walls was peeling in many places, the carpets underfoot pitiable, threadbare. The furniture, scratched and dented over the years, looked as worn out as she felt. Even the china didn't match. Anyone who came into their home knew immediately the impoverished state they lived in.

It was unlikely the eunuchs could be convinced with promise for payment. But there must be a way to bribe them.

The maidservant had heard the commotion and came in looking askance at her. Elena knew she wasn't here for her sake, though. Everyone in the household would want to know if their wages would be paid, as her husband kept promising. Now they would all know Robert had gambled away what little money remained. It was no secret that the servants had been collecting bets on the span of her husband's life. Robert played a dangerous game. He was a foreigner here and easily swindled out of their pittance. This wasn't calm and proper England but a hostile land with hostile natives.

The smaller man said something in Turkish to her husband. She wasn't used to the language and only recognized smatterings. None of what they said made sense. Robert ran a hand through his hair, his words careful as he asked them in his most authoritative voice—sorely lacking in a tone of command since the devolution of their old life—to leave his home.

The one who had spoken shook his head and placed his hand on his hip, perilously close to the bloodred handle of his scimitar. An ominous sign.

Elena swallowed what little saliva she had and watched her husband's Adam's apple bob. The eunuchs weren't moving. Robert's only reaction was to clench his jaw and take a step away from them—clearly done arguing on her behalf. Giving up on her so easily.

It shouldn't surprise her. Still, she fought tears of sadness for how little she meant to the man who had shared the last five years with her. It didn't matter any longer that he'd secured their marriage through deception, cornering her in Lady Aberney's study, approaching her with a wicked gleam in his eye. She was won, so he must have lost fun in the chase after that night.

The silent guard looked to her. Elena stared him in the eye, unwilling to cower before the eunuchs who on further assessment could only be slave traders, not palace guards.

She was safe in her own home. She had to be. She would *not* leave. She made that resolve clear as she looked at him. But it was lost. The eunuch's eyes held no expression. No pity, no sympathy for what her husband had done. Those were the empty, soulless eyes of a man who had seen and lived a hard mercenary life in a world with too many cruelties to keep a compassionate heart for those less fortunate—she being the less fortunate.

She was a noblewoman. They couldn't possibly mean to take her! How could they take her away from her baby?

Forcing her gaze away from the eunuch she glared at her husband. "What of the silver, Robert?" There were candlesticks that could be melted down, some cutlery, too. Was that enough to send these ruffians on their way?

Robert stepped toward her. Looking to the maidservant, he jerked his head in a violent fashion that had the woman leaving the room posthaste. Elena could imagine the maid's whispered words to the rest of the serving staff. Would they stay on after this? She really didn't care. She needed to sort all this nonsense out so she could hold her son. She would fix this. She always fixed her husband's blunders.

He stood before her, looking down but not meeting her gaze. One hand grasped her shoulder; he gave it the smallest squeeze in reassurance. It was lost in the gravity of the situation. "Listen to me, Elena. I've had a bad turn of luck—"

She snapped her head to the side as though struck by his words and glowered. He found some courage to look her in the eye when she let out a hiss of air between her teeth.

"You've always had a bad turn, Robert! You promised me you wouldn't fall into old habits!" She pounded her palm against the seat. "You promised me a new life when our son was born." Her fingers clutched the edge of the settee, grasping for any sort of balance to her lopsided, unfair life.

"I know. And I did keep that promise, Elena. I restricted my outings to a gentleman's establishment. Ali Admen came in for a round of loo with a mutual friend, so I agreed to sit for a hand. I was doing well and stayed on at the table. A little blunt would have not been remiss." He shook his head as though recalling the exact moment of his downfall. "Before I knew it, luck wasn't about me."

She took a deep breath. She must remain calm. Even though the voice in her mind screamed for her to get out of here. As fast as possible. A dread was building in her blood that she would be taken away from her son. God knew what else they'd do to her. Bile rose in her throat. She closed her eyes, breathed in deep through her nose and out through her mouth. She clenched her hands so tight into the seat she thought she'd tear right through the material.

"You *always* lose," she said between gritted teeth. "I will *not* go with them."

I will take my son and head back to England the moment you turn your back, you swine.

"Elena . . ."

"I mean it, Robert. They'll have to drag me out of here." Her voice caught on those words, and she had to force out the next, "I *refuse* to go anywhere."

Eyes flooding with angry tears, she *really* looked at the man who was supposed to be her husband. How could he do this and without so much as a shrug? Was she so worthless?

"Please, Elena." Again with his hand swept through his hair, never a good sign when his agitation got the better of him. "I'll talk to Ali Admen's man of affairs tomorrow. We'll work out another arrangement. We cannot afford . . ."

"No! You disgust me, Robert. What made you think you made a morally sound judgment wagering your own wife for a hand of cards? How dare you! I will not leave. This is my home. In case you've forgotten, our son needs us. He needs *me*." She pressed her clenched fist to her heart, voice breaking on a sob. "You would take away his mother?"

Elena trained her eyes on the larger and quieter of the eunuchs. His expression held nothing useful for her. She stared into those mud-brown eyes and wondered how to mend this before falling into the snare of those deep wells.

The sound of the baby crying had her on her feet and at the door in a trice. *This was her chance. She'd leave Constantinople and never look back.*

"Elena—"

She glanced sidelong at Robert, hand already around the door latch her heart tripping faster than ever as she looked at her husband for the last time. She had to leave here as quickly as her feet could carry her.

"If you think for one moment I'll let Jonathan cry through your good-for-nothing *negotiations*, you're mistaken. You can take my place in their slave quarters until you fix this! I'll be with the baby, should you come to your senses and wish to make amends."

One of the eunuchs grasped the base of her neck, and spun her painfully around. As he pushed her to the closed door, all the air whooshed from her lungs. Her shoulder ached from its impact against the molding. She refused to cry out her pain and bit her lip till she thought it would bleed.

Realization dawned as she tried to dislodge his hand unsuccessfully; he could snap her just like this. Hopefully, she was worth more alive than dead. His hand was unrelenting and with his weight behind it, it proved almost impossible to drag any air into her lungs.

She tried to squirm out of his grasp. She brought her hands up to his chest to push him away but his grip tightened, his body pressing hard and heavily into her, rendering her powerless to move. Deep down, she knew there was never a hope for escape. Why she attempted it, she didn't know. Foolish bravery, perhaps.

No. She attempted it for her son. *Her son. God, what would happen to her son?*

A thin knife rasped against her flesh and jabbed into the vein that beat a furious tempo above the eunuch's thumb. It was the only thing to stop her from pushing at him again. Nothing more than the threat of the sharp tip held her down, the still weight of an ox standing behind that deadly pinprick. Her hands dropped to her side in defeat.

If she were dead, she wouldn't be able to help her son.

The eunuch loosened his grip. From her peripheral vision she saw his other hand swoop down toward her temple. She ducked the blow too late.

"She'll fetch a pretty price. She has nice form. Skin's tight and free of blemish."

The tall, thin Englishman was the one who spoke, his spectacles resting on the end of his nose as he pinched various parts of her flesh in his inspection. His touch was light but no less invasive than some of the crueler handlings she'd had over the days. It angered her that he talked as though she were a fine piece of horseflesh and not a human being.

This was the same man who'd looked her over three days ago. The first Englishman she'd seen in this pit worse than any hell imaginable. She'd begged his help then, tried pleading that her being here was a grave misunderstanding. Told him that the life of her baby rested on his goodwill.

He hadn't listened. So Elena said nothing, just bit her lip to still her shaking. She wanted to cry when he prodded at her naked breasts and touched her bare stomach through the tear in her chemise. No sense in crying out. That would earn her another beating. She'd given up begging for help days ago—or was it a week? Time was irrelevant, days leached into night then back into day. No one cared about her here. She was just another slave in their dark, cold gazes.

When she had awoken in this dilapidated warehouse the first thing she noticed was the dingy faded ashen walls. When her head had stopped throbbing she was nauseatingly assaulted with the smell of unwashed human bodies. The stench of excrement and urine so thick in the air it was as though it had sunk into the very foundation of the building. When she breathed through her mouth she tasted that awful, stale reek of dirty human bodies. Better to smell that rotten stench.

Heavy muslin over the large windows stopped the light from reaching its warm rays out to her and blocked fresh air from cleaning out her aching lungs. The slave handlers bound her with thick rope, looping it through a rusted metal collar that tethered to the wall. She'd been treated like an animal since her arrival. Poked, jabbed, humiliated with their scrutiny and quibbling of a price over her.

She should be happy they hadn't completely forgotten her like some of the other slaves huddled in their own reek and filth. They gave her a grayish sludge they called food once a day. Sometimes there was rice or pilaf, which she'd refused at first. But after a couple days of dire hunger, she'd learned to close her eyes and eat around the cockroaches infesting the food. She pretended the wriggling of their bodies was merely a product of her overactive imagination.

Every man who looked her over had torn more of the meager clothes she wore, all in an effort to see her in the flesh. She tried to cover the exposed parts, but it did her no good. Most of her nightclothes were shredded or gone. All that remained was her undershirt and drawers, soiled from the grime crusted on every surface. They'd even taken her slippers and stockings. Her left heel had blistered something fierce on the first day, when she'd tripped over the chain nailed into the floor.

At first, she'd begged and cried that they spare her some privacy. All to no avail. Having had enough of her antics, the guard had hit her so hard in the stomach she'd fallen over gasping for air. The pain still bothered her, a low persistent ache, but it lessened as the purplish bruises faded to an unsightly green. She had learned her lesson that night. Now she only cried out her misery when the slaves bedded down on the hard earth at night. She didn't beg to be released after that, realizing they might do worse next time. If they did treat her any worse, she might never escape. Not that she knew *how* she would escape.

"Yes, but she's used goods. They don't like their women in *this* state in the high court."

The other man said this and then grasped one of her engorged breasts, squeezing the areola and nipple until milk flowed down her torso. She let out a cry of distress and pain with the release of built-up fluid. Mostly it was a cry against the abject humiliation of being handled in such a fashion. That milk was for her child. Her child that she might never see again.

God, she did not belong here. She could not survive here much longer.

Her whimpers had the slave guard yanking the rope around her neck, forcing her to silence as she was pulled back a step. She wedged her fingers beneath the collar so she could breathe. Her neck probably sported the same bruising displayed on her abdomen. It ached and itched so much from the incessant tugging and sweating through the hot days.

She stood as tall and straight as she could and stared defiantly at the two men. Could they see the hatred in her eyes? The English one looked at her thoughtfully. Assessingly. She didn't like the flicker in his gaze; it looked too much like desire. It repulsed her to be looked upon so lecherously. What did they think to do with her?

Then their words registered. High court. Did they mean to purchase her for the Sultan? She wouldn't cooperate with any of them; she was English, not some slave they could do whatever they pleased with. Though if one were to look upon her now for the first time, they'd see nothing but a dirty, half-naked woman taking on the stink of a chamber pot. Her skin was crusted with dirt. She couldn't even scrape the soil out from under her nails, as much as she tried. Even the beautiful curls of her hair hung limp, greasy and tangled around her like a banshee's wild mane.

She'd been forced into something less honorable than her worth. Made worse because any attempt to stand up for herself would earn her another beating. She didn't think they cared whether she lived or died. It made her want to fight, to scream, to hurt these men who treated a human so low. These men kept her away from her child. She despised them.

The Englishman called over the slave trader, whom she now knew was Ali Admen, the devil her husband had wagered all but his soul to. He sat at a great wooden table conducting a transaction with a Turk. When he rose, he strode toward them on light, silent steps. A trained warrior would walk in this manner, as if on the very air. Silly thought that, but her mind had taken some unusual turns these few days. Bound to happen being deprived food, water and any privacy to spare a scrap of her modesty, or her sanity for that matter.

The older man said something in Turkish. She only caught a few words: *private* and *goods*. And those two words were enough to frighten her. She shrank back a small step. The slave handler didn't notice this time, so did not reprimand her with another tug.

She didn't want to be under their scrutiny any more.

The buyer wanted to look her over. In private. Others had left the main area under force and were taken to the door at the far end of the room——she heard their whimpering, crying, and sometimes their screams. All from no more than a dozen feet away. She didn't want to know what happened in there.

Why didn't one of her servants come and find her? Had her husband still not paid them? Surely one of them would be kind enough to spare her this evil, this life she didn't belong to. Wouldn't they help her for her child's sake? Her husband wasn't coming for her; it would be a servant. Otherwise, Robert would have been here days ago. He was probably lost in his cups watching the horse races, losing more money they didn't have.

What was left to barter? Another human being? Their son? He wouldn't dare.

She closed her eyes and made the slave handler drag her to the room. If she could have done it unscathed, she would have dropped to the ground and clawed her hands into the packed earth in pure defiance. But she didn't. The guard would have no compunctions about strangling her to prove his supremacy, her worthlessness.

Once inside, a cursory glance told her the room was empty. Was this a good or a bad sign? She didn't know. There were no windows to escape through should they leave her alone, just four stark walls with lit oil lamps set into them. The guard led her to a wooden bench and motioned her to sit with a jab of his finger. She did as ordered. The guard came around to her side and looped the rope through a metal ring at the end of the bench.

Was that to prevent her from defending herself? She wasn't fool enough to think she could escape this place. She wasn't strong enough. She saw other slaves held down and beaten for disobedience in their desperate attempts to flee.

There had to be another way to escape, someone she could bribe into releasing her. She was desperate. She'd been away from her baby too long. But she had nothing of value to offer for her freedom.

The Englishman stepped into the room saying something commanding to the guard in Turkish. Then he looked her directly in the eye. "I've asked him to leave us in private. Will you behave if you're left unchained?" He spoke English.

Elena swallowed hard and stared up at the Englishman's unforgiving stance. She gave a small nod in agreement. She couldn't run, but she would defend herself with her free hands if he took advantage of her vulnerability.

The guard turned and left. The Englishman came forward with no readable emotion on his face.

Fingers prodding into her neck, he looked over the blisters and scrapes made by the collar. Instinctually, she jerked away, not wanting to be touched. He moved gently. She guessed he didn't want to hurt her more than necessary. Tilting her this way and that, he inspected her cuts and bruises with care. He had her open her mouth so he could check her teeth, his fingers pushing them to see if they were loose or rotted. Nothing was left untouched except the private area between her legs, a small thing to be thankful for. He palmed her dispassionately, kneading around her aching, heavy breasts, under her arms, over her stomach, looking closely at the bruising there and pressing into it. She couldn't help but cry out in pain and hunched forward, protecting her belly.

"Bleeding seems to be on the surface," he said. "That's good."

He lifted her bare feet next, almost toppling her from the bench, to examine them toe by toe. Then he stood to inspect her hair, picking through the knots, looking for lice. She held herself inert and closed her eyes against the degradation. She wanted to remain strong. If she fell apart now, what good was she to her son? But her body was sore, stiff and hurt worse than anything she'd ever experienced.

Her tears fell anyhow.

When he finished, he shuffled back a step and tilted his head to the side in question. "How old are you?"

She didn't answer. Just gave him her most incredulous look through flooded eyes. He had no right to question her, not after she'd begged for his help and made a fool of herself in the process. He had reduced her to an abject slave, throwing herself down at his feet. Begging for the safety of her son, only to be ignored and then punched in the stomach by the guards—who laughed as she cried out for them to stop.

"There are a number of ways we can go about this. So either answer my question, or I'll have you chained to the wall in the slave quarters, where I will inspect you in the public room."

She turned so she could look him in the eye; he was level with her face, one fist planted on the bench beside her thigh. "Four and twenty."

"Old enough"—he pushed off the bench with his fist and walked away from her—"but not too old that this business will grow tiresome and wear your body down."

He said it so bluntly she almost didn't believe the words she heard. *This business.* She had a good estimation what *this business* entailed. And *this business* was not a safe place for her son, nor a place she wanted to be. "Why are you doing this to me? Why won't you help me?"

"I'm not doing anything, dear child. I've looked into your claims. You are who you say. A surprise really. It's not the first time I've heard such a tale."

"Then why am I still chained here like a wild dog?"

"Because you belong to the slave master of this establishment. And now, I wish to purchase you for my employer."

"I belong to no one."

Oh God, what had happened to her family? Her baby? Please, please let Jonathan be safe.

His lip lifted in an arrogant smirk. What wasn't he telling her? The blood pounded in her ears so loudly she almost didn't hear his next words . . .

"I'm sorry to inform you, madam, but your husband is dead, his properties seized."

She gasped. Though she had never professed to love Robert, he *was* her husband. Helpless to stop fresh tears from flowing, she bowed her head into her hands, her tears washing away the dirt crusted there. *Dead?* How was that possible? He was part of the embassy here; how ludicrous that someone would harm him. No matter his flaws, he was an English gentleman.

But this wasn't England.

He only mentioned her husband. Could her son still live? Every time she opened her mouth to ask, her voice caught on another sob. She swiped the tears away without success.

He went on. "It seems he didn't make it through his negotiations. I know naught of all the gruesome details, nor do I care to. What I do know is his properties, including you, now belong to Ali Admen. You're to be sold to pay off your late husband's vowels."

Was such a thing possible? Would this country trade in the enslavement of English women? She sucked in a breath and put a hand to her chest as she tried to calm herself. The air was hot and thin in this room, making it difficult to breathe. She needed to know about her child. "What of my son?" She was almost afraid to hear the answer.

"Let us discuss our business before the welfare of your babe."

"How can you be so cruel!" She made to stand but the collar caught and jerked her back down to the bench. She clenched her fists in her lap to still the shaking from the rage and fear building throughout her body.

Was her son well? Was he hurt? She needed to know. She needed to be with him. She took a deep breath; it did nothing to calm her tattered nerves.

He ignored her questions. "I'm here to make you an offer. One which will not only better your future, but also save you from a fate far worse than the one you've lived this past week. I should hate to think what *will* happen should you choose to be difficult."

"How could all this come to pass? How dare you do this!"

"Madam, I dare do nothing. Your husband is the sole person responsible for your current circumstance."

Feeling more bravado than she ought, she said, "And why should I take your offer?"

"I daresay mine comes at a prettier and much more advantageous price than you're likely to find in the bowels of this hovel. I can also offer you the safety of your child." His lip tilted upward the minutest amount in a satisfied sneer.

So that was his bargaining chip. Her cooperation might guarantee her son's safety. Could he really help her son? Did he even know the whereabouts of her child? She clenched her jaw and her fists as she stared up at her nemesis or her savior—one and the same at this point. Could she trust him? She was at a grave disadvantage. How was she to know if her son was even alive?

"How can I trust you?" Or anyone for that matter. Her own husband, sworn to protect her, had sold her to this fate.

This might be her last chance to see her son while they both lived. If she stayed here much longer, she wouldn't survive the handling some of the other slaves endured. Not in the long run. It was only a matter of time before they treated her like a mongrel, good to no one but for beating out their frustrations.

"You can't trust my words. Nor do I expect you to. I'll make you a generous offer."

"Feeling charitable to a white slave, are you?"

The heavy weight of despair constricted her—suffocated her. He didn't even flinch at her words. She didn't care. It was hard to hold her tongue when death stared her in the eye daily. Eventually, she knew she'd beg for the end staying here.

"I'm employed by a wealthy man, madam. His sole indulgence is his harem. I would ask you to become one of his harem girls . . . in exchange for the safety of your son."

She stopped breathing altogether and repeated the words in her head. Could she really be hearing this right? A harem girl? A harlot? Is this what her husband had managed to reduce her life to—to become the plaything of some strange man in the hopes of saving *their* child?

She dropped her head into her hands and cried from the hopelessness of the situation. For the life she once knew, knowing it was no longer for her. She cried for her son, who would grow up with a whore for a mother if she agreed to this madness.

Should she agree to this? How could she not? There was no other option. Her tears came harder and faster with every despairing thought.

The Englishman waited quietly for her to compose herself.

She was to find her way alone. To sell her body for her son's safety.

No one would even note her absence from society. Now her only escape from this slave trade was in sexual servitude. Rubbing the last of the tears away, she looked up to the only salvation left to her and Jonathan. His arms were braced, his expression blank as he leaned on the far wall, standing calmly as he awaited her decision.

She bowed her head and stared at her lap. "Will your employer be kind to my son?" Her voice was so faint she almost didn't recognize it as her own.

It was her son's welfare that mattered now. She would sacrifice her comfort a hundred times over for her child. Without Jonathan, there was nothing left to live for.

"If *you* obey him, he'll have no reason to cause harm to either of you. He takes great pride in his harem and business. You've no need to fear him. He does not abuse his women, nor do I imagine he would abuse a child. He doesn't have any so I cannot say for sure."

Could she ask for more assurance than that? She could take this offer and what may come may come. Or she could rot in this hell on earth and never see her son again. She licked at her dry, cracked lips. "Why me?"

"Ah, there are many reasons for that, madam."

"Am I to guess your reasoning, then?"

"My employer has a certain fondness for English women with dark skin. Imagine my surprise when I happened upon you speaking the Queen's English in its dulcet, educated tone in this place. You'll also fetch a fair price from the other lords who visit his pleasure island. But only after he's trained you to do your duties as one of his harem girls."

Her stomach flipped. Elena raised her hand to her head to massage her temple, hoping it would help her find balance in a suddenly spinning room. She was to be a sex slave. Not just the whore for one amoral man but the sex slave for a plethora of men.

She looked up and focused on the Englishman. "If I agree to your offer . . . will you take me out of this place and reunite me with my child?"

He nodded. "Are you agreed?"

She couldn't swallow past the lump in her throat to ease the tension tightening her body, threatening to hyperventilate her. She nodded her yes. With that nod she threw away any hope of comfort. There was no other choice. She did this to protect her son.

She felt so helpless and despondent that the last bit of spirit in her heart—once so strong and determined to make something of the unfair life she'd been given—withered away. She was the wounded deer looking into the predatory eyes of a wolf, knowing this was it. This was all that was left. Do or die—what choice was there in that? What fairness lay in this world? None.

He pushed himself from the wall, still expressionless. "Then, my dear, I'm off to haggle a decent price for you."

Elena hung her head in shame. What had she agreed to? God save her if this was the wrong decision for her son.

Sara Lindsey

A lifelong bibliophile and history buff, Sara Lindsey graduated from Scripps College with an Art History major, but too many unpaid museum internships had taught Sara that The Arts did not pay. At least, not the kind of money that would support her obsession with Prada purses... So she decided to become a doctor.

While looking at medical schools, Sara realized that what she really wanted to do was write... Well, what she really wanted to do was marry a handsome lord with a palatial estate, but since aristocrats are hard to come by, Sara decided to use her imagination and live vicariously through her heroines instead.

She currently divides her time between her native Los Angeles and Manhattan, where she is pursuing her graduate degree in information and library science. Having read a number of romances featuring librarians, Sara figures this profession bodes well for someday getting her own happily ever after. In the meantime, she plans to turn as many unsuspecting library patrons as possible into fellow romance addicts.

You can find out more about Sara by visiting her website at http://www.saralindsey.net.

Praise for Sara

"This novel is charming beyond belief, with vibrant characters, polished and fresh writing, and one of the most adorable heroines you'll ever meet. Read *Promise Me Tonight*, and get ready to fall in love!"
   —Lisa Kleypas, *New York Times* bestselling author

"Fans of Julia Quinn will find much that is familiar and enjoyable in Lindsey's debut."
   —*Publishers' Weekly*

"A marvelous debut and perfect introduction to a promising series about the Weston siblings."
   —Kristin Ramsdell, *Library Journal*

Promise Me Tonight

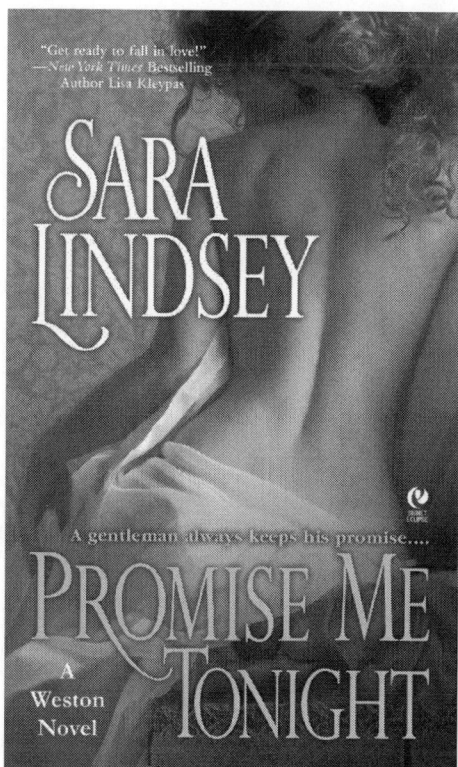

"Get ready to fall in love!"
—*New York Times* Bestselling
Author Lisa Kleypas

SARA
LINDSEY

A gentleman always keeps his promise....

PROMISE ME
A
Weston
Novel
TONIGHT

Isabella is determined to marry James...

Isabella Weston has loved James Sheffield for as long as she can remember. Her come-out ball seems the perfect chance to make him see her in a new light.

James is determined never to marry...

James is stunned to find the impish girl he once knew has blossomed into a sensual goddess. And if he remembers his lessons, goddesses always spell trouble for mortal men.

A compromise is clearly necessary.

When Izzie kisses James, her artless ardor turns to a masterful seduction that drives him mad with desire. But, no stranger to heartbreak, James is determined never to love, and thus never to lose. Can Isabella convince him that a life without love might be the biggest loss of all?

Available February 2, 2010, from Signet
ISBN-10: 0451229371 ✳ISBN-13: 978-0451229373

Chapter One

Dere Dear Mama,
   I am ~~gowing~~ going to marry James. It will be ~~nise~~ nice. We will live
   near you. I am ~~hape~~ happy. I love you.
Love, Isabella
(*Mises Danyels helpd me with the speling.*)
      —From the correspondence of Miss Isabella Weston, age six

Letter to her mother, Mary, Viscountess Weston, expounding on the
benefits to be found in marrying the boy next door—August 1784

WESTON MANOR, ESSEX
JULY 1792

Perched precariously on the banister of the long portrait gallery so as to
better observe the party in progress one floor below, fourteen-year-old
Isabella Weston was faced with the devastating sight of her true love dancing
with another woman. She turned her head to look at one of her younger sisters,
Olivia, who, safely seated on the floor, was craning her head to peer through
the carved marble balusters.

   "Can you believe how that—that *hussy* is dancing with *James?*" Izzie
demanded. "Honestly, she should be ashamed, dancing like that with a man
who is not her husband."

   Izzie, of course, fully planned on dancing with James Sheffield that way,
but she would be married to him when she did—or engaged, at the very least.

Of course, since she'd been planning the wedding since the day they'd met, Isabella felt they *were* practically engaged.

She'd been only six when they'd met, but one smile from James had been all it took for her to tumble head over heels in love. Of course, she hadn't really known at the time that it was *love*—just that she wanted him more than she'd ever wanted anything before. She wanted to take care of him, to share her family with him, to fill his world with laughter and brightness, and banish the shadows from his eyes. And though she'd been young, Izzie had been nothing if not determined, and she'd determined right then and there that someday when she was all grown-up, James Sheffield would be hers. Now she *was* all grown-up, or *almost*, and the sight of James with another woman made that "almost" *almost* unbearable.

"Oh, Izzie." Livvy sighed, sounding far older than her twelve years. "Not James *again*!"

Isabella shrugged. "I can't help it. I love him."

"I know. Believe me, *I know*. I would get far more sleep if you didn't. But he, well—" Olivia bit her lip and tugged at a lock of golden brown hair. "He's older."

"James is *not* old. He just turned twenty in May. Hal"—she waved a hand at the crowd below that included the girls' older brother, Henry—"will be twenty in September, and he certainly isn't old."

"I didn't say James was old, I said he was *older*. And he's Hal's best friend ... and our neighbor. To him you're nothing more than a little sister, and even if he *is* aware of your feelings, I'm worried that—"

"Aargh! I just saw *that woman* touch his—" Izzie waved a hand in the vicinity of her backside, nearly toppling over the railing as she did so. As much as she wanted to squash *that woman* like a bug, she had imagined doing so in a more metaphorical sense. And, of course, such a fall might well break her neck and, if it didn't, her mother might kill her anyway for appearing *en déshabillé* in front of the guests. Not that her thick flannel nightgown and wrapper didn't cover every inch of her from the neck down, because they did, but it wouldn't be *proper*.

Along with snakes, spiders and apricot jam, Izzie loathed the word "proper." Henry tormented her with the former, her mother with the latter. But it was her mother's sort of torture that made her quake in her boots; propriety and Izzie had never gone together.

Izzie hopped down from the banister and plopped herself beside her sister. "Now, what were you worried about?"

"Nothing," Livvy muttered.

"Do you know who she is?"

Olivia rolled her eyes, and without bothering to ask for clarification as to the "she" in question, replied, "I believe the woman dancing with James is the rather notorious widow who finally convinced Lord Finkley to walk down the aisle again."

"Oh dear," Isabella whispered, torn between fascination and dismay.

After his wife had passed away some fifty years earlier, Lord Finkley had spent his time with a parade of young mistresses and society widows, each of whom had hoped to seduce the wealthy elderly man into matrimony. None had succeeded … until now. This meant that James was either in the hands of the most cunning female England had seen in half a century or of an evil sorceress—or both. Either way, Izzie didn't like it one bit!

"I had expected something more of the woman who finally trapped Lord Finkley."

Olivia shook her head. "You're just jealous, and you know it."

"The way she's acting is disgraceful," Izzie huffed. "Do you *see* the way she's throwing herself at him? Why doesn't her husband *do* something?"

"Because he's in the corner, snoring his head off, and has been for the last hour?" Livvy suggested. "Truly, I don't think James minds. She *is* quite beautiful," she added, rather unnecessarily in Izzie's opinion.

"I suppose. If you like the tall, skinny, far–too–much–bosom–on–display sort."

Of course, even though she would have liked to, Izzie couldn't blame the woman for throwing herself at James. He was too handsome for his own good. She could spend—drat it, *had spent*—countless hours cataloging his physical perfections, the first of which had to be his hair.

It was the color of vintage brandy, highlighted with gold where the sun had kissed it. He wore it just a bit longer than the current fashion, and it curled up at the ends where it met his collar.

Then there were his eyes, beautiful green eyes fringed by lashes that were most unfairly longer and darker than hers. *Her* lashes were a scant shade darker than the straw–colored hair on her head, and didn't that just figure. Vanity, thy name is Isabella Weston.

He had a nicer nose than she did, too. Aquiline, she believed, was the word, and it made him look quite fierce and arrogant in a way she secretly found thrilling. Her nose was very average in comparison. It wasn't even fashionably *retroussé* like Olivia's. And wasn't that the height of unfairness? Isabella felt that as the first daughter born in the Weston family, she ought to have had first pick of nice noses.

Lady Finkley had a rather elegant nose, Isabella noted unhappily. It was a trifle on the long side, though, she decided as Lady Finkley leaned close to James and whispered something in his ear that caused him to throw his head back with laughter.

Isabella ground her teeth as the clock in the gallery sounded half-past eleven. James and Henry had promised to bring sweets up to her and Livvy before midnight since the girls were too young to be allowed downstairs for the ball.

Olivia yawned. "I'm sorry, Izzie, but I can't stay awake any longer. They've probably forgotten about us in any case. I'm for bed. Good night."

"Mmm—hmmm," Isabella mumbled, never taking her eyes off the scene below.

"Common courtesy demands that you wish me good night in return."

"Mmm—hmmm."

Olivia gave a loud huff. "The things I have to put up with," she muttered under her breath. Izzie heard her, but she was too preoccupied to give her sister a worthy parting shot. Livvy heaved a disgusted sigh as she stood and padded off toward the bedchamber they shared.

The things I have to put up with, indeed, Isabella thought as she watched James walk with Lady Finkley around the perimeter of the ballroom, her arm wrapped about his and his hand resting on the small of her back. Izzie grimaced. She knew exactly how powerful that touch was. It was so magical that from the very first time she had held his hand, she'd never wanted to let go. She did, however, want Lady Finkley to let go. In fact, she just plain wanted her to *go.* Finally, after two immeasurably long turns about the room, Izzie's wish came at least partly true when James escorted Lady Finkley over to her comatose spouse.

Izzie tracked James as he moved through the throng of guests, pausing when she caught sight of her parents dancing together, gazing at each other as if they were the only people in the room. It was sweet, she supposed, that they were still so much in love, but it was also rather embarrassing! It was a trifle discomfiting, too, given that Isabella's baby brother, Richard, had been christened just that morning—thus the reason for the celebration downstairs—and her mother had said, with a pointed look toward Isabella's father, that she did *not* plan on there being any more christenings at Weston Manor until she was a grandmother. However, the looks she was currently giving her husband told an entirely different story!

Not really wanting to follow where that train of thought led, Isabella's eyes sought out James once more and found him with Henry, who was standing in the crush of people by the refreshments. She should have known. Her mother often said her eldest child had been born with a bottomless pit in place of a stomach. Unfortunately the same could be said of Lord Blathersby, whose sole interest in life—besides food, of course—was his sheep, which meant that Henry often got stuck speaking with the ovine–loving gentleman. From the pained look on her brother's face, he'd been trapped for some time now. *Poor Hal. But,* she thought in true sisterly fashion, *better him than me!*

James Sheffield had always considered himself a good person, but he spent several moments savoring his best friend's suffering expression before going in to rescue him from the most boring man in Christendom.

"Took you bloody long enough," Henry grumbled as the two men made their escape. "I've been trying to get your attention for ages, but you were too wrapped up in the luscious Lady Finkley to pay any notice. Not that I blame you. Had similar thoughts myself. Bloody unfair, though, that you got to play Casanova while I was stuck with old Blathersby and his sheep."

"Blathersby and his sheep." James laughed. "Never fear; I've heard it all before and on multiple occasions." He shook his head. "Come, it's nearly midnight and we promised Izzie and Livvy we'd bring them some sweets."

Henry grimaced. "Lord, it completely slipped my mind. Good thing you remembered. You know how Izzie gets when she's angry."

James nodded and hustled Henry over to the crowd waiting to get at the dessert table.

"What a devilishly dull affair," Henry remarked as they waited in line. "First the christening this morning, and now this. It was good of you to come. You could have been off weeks ago."

"Of course I came," James replied, a gruff note creeping into his voice. "Neither of us would have been comfortable leaving until your mother was safely delivered, and delaying our trip for another month made no real difference. The Coliseum isn't going anywhere, and it was important to your mother that you be here for Richard's christening."

"And you," Henry insisted.

"Only to make sure I keep you out of trouble," James teased, but his chest was tight with emotion. The Westons were the closest thing he had to a family since he'd been orphaned at age ten and sent to live with his grandfather, the Earl of Dunston. The best that could be said of the earl was that his main property, Sheffield Park, neighbored Weston Manor, home to Viscount Weston and his family.

They had taken him in as another son; their warm, bustling home had been his refuge. When he and Henry had gone off to Eton, Lady Weston had kissed and clucked and wept over both of them, a performance she had repeated when they'd headed to Oxford.

She had cried when they'd graduated earlier that year, but James figured that was primarily because Henry had spent more time "rusticating" than he had at school. James had taken a First in Literature, partly to please Lady Weston who was more than a little enamored of a certain Elizabethan playwright. Henry had joked that morning that if his father had not had some say in naming them, the family's newest addition might well have been christened Hamlet or Falstaff. Yes, Richard was fortunate to have such a father. James had once thought himself lucky in his own sire, but—

He shook his head. He didn't want to think about it. Not tonight. Not ever, really. Better to focus on the present, and—

"Put it back on the plate, Hal. These are for Izzie and Livvy," James scolded as they filed past the refreshments table.

"When did you grow eyes in the back of your head?" Henry grumbled through a mouthful of cake.

"I've known you since we were ten. Don't you think a decade of friendship gives me some insight? Besides, you eat everything within reach."

"I'm a growing lad," Henry retorted.

James chuckled. He was tall at six feet, but his best friend had at least three inches on him and was built like a brawny prizefighter.

"If you grow any bigger, I am going to sell you to a traveling Gypsy circus."

"Remind me once more why we are friends."

"Aside from the fact that no one else would put up with you?" James joked, turning to look back at Henry. "For one thing, you would never have graduated without my help."

Henry laughed. "I still can't puzzle out how you went to all those boring lectures."

"Self-control?" James suggested.

Henry grinned and shrugged his shoulders. "I doubt it would have made a difference. I was never much good at lessons."

James couldn't argue with that. Intellectual pursuits were not, admittedly, Henry's forte. Bedroom games—actually, games and sports in general—were where he excelled. Still, James was certain Henry was smarter than he let on;

his best friend certainly wasn't lacking in imagination, he reflected, remembering all of the scrapes Henry had gotten them into.

He was smiling as he made his way up to the gallery, Henry right behind him, but his amusement faded when he saw Isabella standing at the top of the stairs, one foot tapping impatiently, her arms crossed.

"Finally!" she exclaimed. "I was beginning to think you weren't coming."

Standing as she was, the braces of candles flanking the staircase illuminated her from behind, casting a golden glow all about her and gilding her unruly blonde curls into a halo. She looked like an irate angel.

"What happened to Livvy?" Henry asked.

Izzie gave them both a pointed look. "*She* got tired of waiting, figured you had forgotten us, and decided to go to bed."

Henry looked down at the plate and glass in his hands as the clock chimed the quarter hour. "I'm sure she's still up. I'll go take this to her. Wouldn't want her to think we forgot. She can be nearly as bad as you." And with that said, he took off down the hallway.

"What does he mean, 'She can be nearly as bad as you'?" Izzie muttered, sitting down.

"Er, have some cake," James said quickly, shoving the plate of sweets at her. He waited until she'd downed three gingersnaps and a piece of cake before deeming her mood restored enough for him to safely sit beside her.

"So, did you enjoy the dancing?" he asked.

"Not as much as you seemed to," she said, a hint of bitterness shading the words.

"Beg pardon?" James leaned closer to her, certain he'd misheard her.

"I simply remarked that you seemed to be having a grand time dancing with Lady Finkley." She stared down at her plate. "Is she your lover?"

"W-what?" James sputtered. "Izzie! That—that is totally inappropriate. You shouldn't even *know* about—"

"Lovers?" she supplied, gazing up impishly at him as she licked her fingers.

"Yes, blast it! You shouldn't know about those sorts of things, and you certainly shouldn't ever speak of them."

"Then she isn't?" Isabella queried.

"No!" James exploded, and then lowered his voice. "Dash it all, this isn't proper. And it certainly isn't any of your business."

"Oh."

The softly uttered syllable contained a definite note of dejection. She looked away, and James thought he saw her shoulders tremble. He instantly gentled his tone. "Izzie, look at me. Come on. *Izzie.*"

She kept her eyes glued to the plate in her hands. He took it from her and set it aside, then placed a finger under her chin, raising her head until he could look into her eyes.

"My God, you're *jealous*," he said incredulously. She swung her head away but made no attempt to deny it. James cupped his hand around her cheek, turning her face back to his, and felt wetness on the silky, soft flesh pressed to his palm. He watched a single tear trickle down her pale cheek, then another and another, turning her lashes into dark golden spikes.

"Sweetheart," he pleaded, though he hadn't a clue what he was pleading for. Direction, he supposed. And he had learned from past experience that uttering an endearment was the safest way to break the silence in situations like these. Of course, he had never been in this particular position before, and he hoped never to be in it again. It was damned uncomfortable!

Bloody hell. Isabella had always dogged his heels when she was younger, but he'd had no idea she fancied him in that way. She looked miserable and defeated, so unlike her usual sunny self, and it killed him to be the cause of it. He slung his arm around her shoulders, hugging her close. She burrowed her face into his shoulder, soaking his jacket with her tears.

"Don't cry, Izzie," James begged. "Please, don't cry."

"I-it's j-just that you were s-smiling and laughing with her and I just w-wished so badly that I was older and could wear a beautiful gown and be the one dancing with you." The words were muffled as they poured out against the soft, black wool of his coat. He murmured nonsense into her hair, soothing her as he would an upset child, but it only made her cry harder.

"Hush, now." James cupped her face in his hands and wiped her tears away. "I am not nearly so good a dancer as to be worth all this fuss."

The small smile she gave him made James feel like the king of England—utterly grand and slightly mad. As James stared into her watery eyes, for a moment, it seemed as if he saw his soul gazing back at him; the thought terrified him, and he pulled his hands away as if burned.

"Someday," he said gruffly, "when you're older and have that beautiful dress, there will be so many men wanting to dance with you, you'll wonder why you wanted to dance with *me*."

"That is *not* true!" Isabella protested fervently. "I will want to dance with you for the rest of my life. Only you. I know it. I *know*, and I won't change my mind. I *won't*."

"You *will*," James insisted.

"Never." She sniffed and shook her head mutinously. "I lo—"

"I hope you are not so foolish as to think yourself in love with me."

She flinched at his tone.

He hated that he was hurting her, but it was best to end this infatuation now. "What you feel for me isn't love—affection, admiration even, but not love. And if you're smart you will save your love for some lucky man who deserves it and will love you back. I am not capable of love."

"But surely, when you were younger..."

"That was a long time ago. I have had some years, and no small amount of help from my grandsire, in which to conquer that weakness."

Isabella shot to her feet. "Love is *not* a weakness—"

"For God's sake, lower your voice." He stood and looked down at her. "So young and innocent," he murmured. "Izzie, I hope you will never find love to be a weakness." His voice was weary and bleak. "But I promise you it can be."

She shook her head mutinously and jabbed a finger at his chest. "And I promise you I will still want that dance."

James sighed.

Izzie glowered, her bottom lip thrust out and quivering, and he knew the fight was up. "All right, don't glare at me so. If you still wish it, when the time is right, I will certainly claim that dance."

Isabella's face brightened, and her eyes lit with sudden hope.

James felt a moment of trepidation, but he told himself it was foolish. Izzie would likely fix her attention on some other gentleman and forget this entire exchange within a fortnight. And if she didn't, it wasn't as though a dance with her would change anything.

"Do you promise?" Isabella demanded.

"Promise what?" Henry asked, his sudden presence startling them both.

"James was just going to promise to dance with me at my come-out ball," Isabella replied.

He hadn't been about to do any such thing, James wanted to protest, but he didn't want Henry to know what had transpired. For one thing, it would embarrass Izzie. For another, he wasn't certain how Hal would react.

He might take it as a great joke; Henry was generally an easy-going fellow. When it came to his family, though, Henry was all seriousness—fierce, protective, pistols-at-dawn seriousness. Of course, James had done nothing to encourage Izzie, but Henry might not care. And James really didn't want to get laid flat because of some innocent fancy. From their sparring sessions at Gentleman Jackson's, James was painfully aware that Henry had a bruising right hook.

"Izzie, your come-out ball?" Henry frowned. "That's years from now and—"

"I promise," James said quietly, his eyes never leaving Isabella's.

"Good." Isabella gave James a smile that had him wondering if a dance was truly all he had agreed to. He wasn't sure why, but he had the eerie feeling that he had just given himself into the custody of a girl with eyes the color of a summer sky and a smile that filled his heart in a way that scared him down to his toes.

Tempting the Marquess

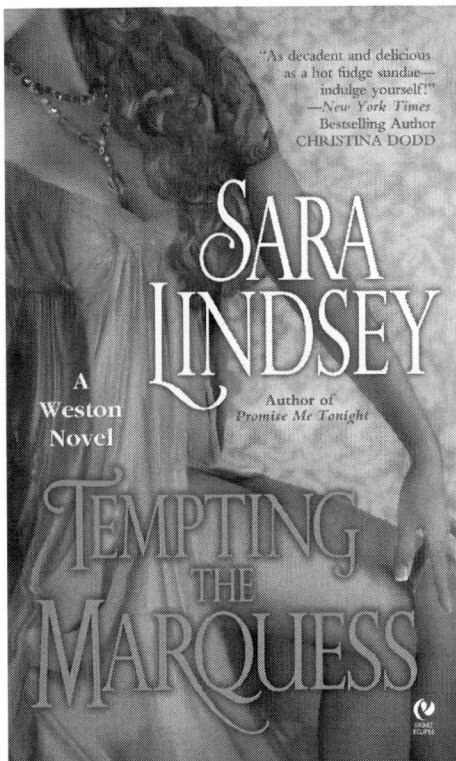

"As decadent and delicious
as a hot fudge sundae—
indulge yourself!"
—*New York Times*
Bestselling Author
CHRISTINA DODD

SARA
LINDSEY

A
Weston
Novel

Author of
Promise Me Tonight

TEMPTING
THE
MARQUESS

The Weston siblings have been blessed with Shakespearean names and an affinity for impropriety. Prepare to fall in love while discovering how the Westons are won.

While Olivia Weston loves matchmaking and romantic novels, she intends to make a suitable match. But first she wants an adventure, and when given the opportunity to visit a reclusive widower living in a haunted castle, Livvy can't possibly resist.

After his wife's death, Jason Traherne, Marquess of Sheldon, shut his heart to everyone but his son, and until now he has succeeded in maintaining his distance. But there's something about Livvy—her unique blend of sweetness and sensuality—that tempts him beyond all reason.

Though there's nothing suitable about the feelings he inspires in her, Livvy can't help falling for the marquess. But can she persuade him to let go of the past and risk his heart again?

Available June 1, 2010, from Signet
ISBN-10 0451230442 ✳*ISBN-13: 978-0451230447*

Chapter One

"If this were played upon a stage now, I could condemn it as an improbable fiction." —*Twelfth Night*, Act III, Scene 4

Olivia stood before the castle's thick wooden portal, inwardly bracing herself against what lay in wait on the other side. Freezing rain had plastered her shabby traveling gown to her body, and the biting wind whipped at her sodden locks. She thought wistfully of her blue velvet pelisse with the ermine trim, but she had left the garment—and the elegant, easy life it represented—behind when she had chosen to run away rather than marry the lecherous Duke of Devonbridge. And now she was a lowly governess, dependent on the kindness and goodwill of her employer . . . and her new master was purported to have little of either.

A lone wolf howled somewhere out on the misty, moonlit moors that stretched for miles around the isolated edifice. She shivered with cold and fright, wondering if she might not be safer with the wolves than inside the castle's walls. A different sort of beast lay within that impenetrable stone fortress. A caged beast, confined not by chains but by his own despair.

The villagers called him the Mad Marquess, for he had been crazed with grief since the death of his wife some four years past. He eschewed all company . . . not that there were many eager to subject themselves to his foul humor. In the past year alone no fewer than eleven maids had resigned their posts at Castle Arlyss. She'd heard rumors, too, of a centuries-old curse. . . .

Olivia raised her face to the heavens, searching for a sign that this was indeed the path she was meant to travel—that she was meant to save this tormented soul and show his son a mother's love. Lightning flashed and crackled through the night sky, setting her hair on end. The angry rumble of thunder followed close behind.

Stiffening her spine, Olivia raised her fist to knock. Then, all of a sudden, a strong gust of the wind snatched at her sleeve, as if trying to stop her. The air swirled around her, rustling through the dead leaves underfoot.

It seemed to whisper a name.

Her name.

Livvy, it murmured. Livvy . . .

A CARRIAGE BOUND FOR CASTLE ARLYSS, PEMBROKESHIRE, WALES
DECEMBER 1798

"Livvy!"

Olivia opened her eyes and stared unseeing out the coach window. She blinked at the few rays of sunlight that dared penetrate the winter gloom lingering over the southwest of England. She shook her head. The wild, stormy night had vanished, and she was back in her aunt's well-sprung carriage.

A wistful sigh escaped her. The dream had been so real. . . . And now she was back to being ordinary Olivia Weston.

She turned her head to look at her young cousin, Charlotte, who was tugging rather insistently at her sleeve.

"Livvy!"

"What is it?" Livvy asked in as understanding a tone as she could muster. The journey from Scotland to Wales had already taken close to a fortnight, and though she loved Charlotte dearly, the boundless energy of a five-year-old was ill-suited to the close confines of a carriage. Not that Olivia was any stranger to small children. As the third of seven siblings, she knew all about them.

The little girl frowned, tugging at one of her glossy, dark ringlets, then shrugged. "I forget."

Livvy bit back a groan and stifled the urge to tear at her hair, which, to her everlasting disappointment, was neither curly nor dark. Neither was it blond and straight. Olivia's hair was a very ordinary, indeterminate shade of brown, and it had just enough of a wave to always escape its pins and make her look unkempt.

"Livvy?"

"What, Char?"

"I remembered. I had a secret to tell you." Charlotte crossed her arms over her chest and flopped back against the plush squabs with a satisfied smile.

"And?" Olivia prompted. She waited for further elucidation, but none was forthcoming. "Did you wish to tell me this secret you remembered?"

Charlotte thought a moment before shaking her head. "I'll tell Queenie instead."

Queen Anne, a doll in lavish court dress, was Charlotte's most prized possession, a distinction it had held since being unwrapped a few weeks past. Yes, Livvy thought, she had been replaced in her cousin's affections by an inanimate object. How distressing! She consoled herself with the knowledge that her conversational skills far surpassed those of Queenie. Then again, so did a squirrel's. As was her wont, she began composing a list in her head:

Ways in Which I Am Superior to Queenie
1. I can read.
2. I can write.
3. My head is not made of wood.
4. I can breathe.

Hmm, perhaps that last should have been first on her list; it seemed a fairly important distinction. Of course, squirrels also breathed. Maybe she ought to list the ways she was superior to squirrels instead. . . . She stopped herself, wondering if it was possible to go mad from boredom.

Aunt Kate looked up from her book to address her daughter. "Charlotte, I do believe Queenie looks a bit peaked. Perhaps you should both try to rest for a time and let your poor cousin alone."

Charlotte was disgusted by this suggestion. "Mama, Queenie is a doll. How can she rest when her eyes don't close?"

Aunt Kate sighed and peered out the window at the passing scenery. "At least we are getting close to the end. We should arrive tomorrow provided the weather doesn't change—" A choked laugh escaped her. "Dear heavens, that child will be the death of me!"

Livvy glanced at Charlotte, who had apparently decided to take her mother's advice. She was curled into the corner of the carriage, with her feet drawn up under her and her head pillowed against one hand. Her eyes were closed, a beatific smile on her face. Queenie lay in the crook of her free arm— Olivia smothered a laugh as she realized the reason for her aunt's proclamation.

As the doll's eyes did not, as Charlotte had pointed out, close, her enterprising mistress had contrived other means by which Queenie might rest. Raising Queenie's gown up over her head did shield her face from light, but this also exposed the doll's lower half. And while Queenie's ensemble boasted exquisitely detailed garters, stockings, and shoes, it did not apparently run to petticoats.

Ha! Petticoats! There was another way in which she was superior to Queenie and squirrels, too, for Livvy had never encountered a petticoat-wearing squirrel and very much doubted she ever would. The closest she was ever like to come was the stable cat her younger sisters had caught long enough to dress it in a bonnet and christening gown.

Aunt Kate leaned forward and spoke quietly so as not to disturb Charlotte. "I feel I ought to warn you about my stepson."

"Warn me?" Olivia's cheeks grew warm. "I hardly think——"

Her aunt waved a hand dismissively. "Heavens, child, I'm not suggesting anything of that nature. No, I only meant to caution you about the welcome we are like to receive."

"You mentioned Lord Sheldon keeps to himself a great deal of the time. I am not expecting to be met with a grand parade. I wish to inconvenience the marquess as little as possible."

That wasn't precisely true.

If all went to plan, she would put the man to a great deal of trouble. . . .

But that was her secret, one she didn't dare share with present company. Not with Aunt Kate, certainly not with Charlotte, and not even with Queenie, who was by nature most admirably closemouthed.

"Jason," Aunt Kate began, then sighed. "I know I should call him Sheldon, but I can't seem to get my mind round it, no matter that he's held the title for five years now. I suppose his Christian name is rather too familiar for polite conversation, but he has always been Jason to me."

"Did he not have use of a courtesy title?"

"There is one," her aunt admitted, "but most of the heirs would rather do without it." Her eyes sparkled with laughter. "Most understandable, really. Would you like to go through life being addressed as Bramblybum?"

"B-bramblybum?" Olivia burst out laughing. She caught her aunt's sharp glance at Charlotte and lowered her voice. "Surely you are joking."

Aunt Kate shook her head. "The marquisate was created for the ninth Viscount Traherne, who was, I gather, a great personal favorite with James I. The viscount's son, who went on to become the second Marquess of Sheldon, openly disapproved of his sire's, ah, special relationship with the king. The Traherne men have never been ones to keep their opinions to themselves, which perhaps accounts for the dearth of ambassadors and politicians in the family. In any case, the young man's outbursts angered the king, and he might have met a very sorry end had not his father intervened. The viscount begged the king to disregard his son and joked how the boy had been born with nettles stinging his backside. The king's revenge was to bestow a marquisate and an earldom upon the viscount. While his father was alive, the second marquess was known by his courtesy title."

"The Earl of Bramblybum," Livvy whispered, torn between horror and hilarity.

"Earl Bramblybum, actually, but I wouldn't suggest you let that pass your lips once we reach Castle Arlyss. Jason always gets fussed on hearing it. He certainly doesn't use the title for Edward. I have told you about Jason's son, Edward, haven't I? He's nearly seven now and such a dear, sweet boy."

Olivia nodded. She wasn't sure if Aunt Kate had told her about Edward, but she knew about him all the same. But that was part of her secret.

Unconsciously, she bent forward and smoothed her hands over her skirts, her fingers searching out the almost imperceptible bump of the little fichu pin she wore affixed to her garter. The dainty brooch featured a tiny silhouette set in a gold frame surrounded by garnets. The portrait was no bigger than her thumbnail, but the artist had rendered the gentleman's profile in great detail, from the slight curl in the hair at his nape to the soft ruffles of his shirt frills. An elegant man, but Livvy reserved final judgment until she met him in the flesh, which, with any luck, would be on the morrow. Finally, she thought, a little sigh escaping her.

"I'll stop nattering on and let you rest." Aunt Kate's eyes twinkled. "You needn't go take the same drastic measures as poor Queenie and cast your skirts over your face."

"I wasn't— I mean, you weren't—," Livvy stammered out a protest.

"Calm yourself, my dear, I'm only teasing. I know I have a tendency to ramble, especially when I don't have to mind my tongue." She winked and nodded in Charlotte's direction.

A rush of pride swept over Olivia at her aunt's words. In the eyes of Society she was an adult and had been since her eighteenth birthday close to a year earlier. Girls her age, and even some younger, had already had their come-outs this past Season. She should have come out then as well, but her sojourn in Scotland with Aunt Kate, Charlotte, and Livvy's newly married (and freshly abandoned) older sister, Isabella, had lasted longer than expected.

Nine months longer, give or take a little.

Olivia hadn't minded putting off her come-out. She wasn't overly anxious to put herself on the Marriage Mart, and besides, her sister had needed her. That last trumped everything else as far as Livvy was concerned.

Aunt Kate reached forward and patted Olivia's knee. "I've grown accustomed to having you and Izzie around. I was so pleased when you asked to come along with us to Wales. I would have invited you had I known you were so interested in this part of the country."

"I must confess, some of my interest stemmed from wanting to avoid traveling home with Mama, spending countless hours trapped in a carriage listening her expound on some Shakespearean heroine or other."

For as long as Olivia could remember, her mother had been writing a critical work about Shakespeare's heroines. Life in the Weston household was all Shakespeare, all the time, at least when her mother was present. The rest of the family bore it with equanimity—mostly because they tended to ignore her—but over the years her mother's obsession increasingly grated on Livvy's nerves. She adored her mother, really she did, but she could easily do without hearing, at least once a week, as she had for her entire life: "Be not afraid of greatness: some are born great, some achieve greatness, and some have greatness thrust upon them."

Lady Weston particularly enjoyed tailoring her recitations so that each of her children would be familiar with the plays from whence had come their names. Though Olivia resented having Shakespeare's greatness constantly thrust upon her, not for the world would she have hurt her mother's feelings by telling her so. All in all, she felt lucky to have been named for a character in Twelfth Night, which, in her opinion, was one of Shakespeare's more tolerable works, and not only because it was relatively short.

Her younger sisters, identical twins Cordelia and Imogen, were stuck with King Lear and Cymbeline, two plays that were, in Olivia's opinion, entirely too puffed up with melodrama. The first words Richard, her precocious little brother, babbled had sounded suspiciously like: "Now is the winter of our discontent." Portia, the baby of the family, hadn't got much past cooing and gurgling when Livvy had left for Scotland. . . .

She realized with a slight pang that she had missed her youngest sister's first words, and a wave of homesickness swept over her. These past months marked the longest time she had ever been away from her younger siblings.

"What's caused that long face?" Aunt Kate asked. "Have I scared you off with this talk of my stepson? You mustn't let him upset you. He is very changed since the Laura's death, and grief affects us all in different ways. Perhaps, given time. . ." She trailed off, her hopes for the future unspoken but entirely clear.

Olivia wanted to say she knew, or at least had an inkling, of what the marquess had been like before his wife's death—but she could not. Instead she smiled brightly and said, "Then we must do our best to bring some cheer to both him and his son this holiday season. If you don't mind, Aunt Kate, I think I'll read a bit while Char is quiet."

Her aunt laughed. "Yes, living with Charlotte one does learn to seize those rare moments of peace. They certainly don't last long."

Olivia nodded distractedly, already absorbed with her book. Or rather, with the piece of paper hidden inside. In bold, scrawling script were the words—the first clue—that had led her to the brooch, thus prompting her seemingly impromptu journey to Wales—words penned by none other than the Mad Marquess of her dreams.

CASTLE ARLYSS, PEMBROKESHIRE, WALES
DECEMBER 22, 1798

Under his butler's disapproving gaze, Jason Traherne, Marquess of Sheldon, reached for the box of sand on his desk and sprinkled some over the letter he had just completed. He waited a moment for the fine grains to dry the ink before brushing the sand back into the box. He set the paper aside and stood, noting how Gower's shoulders relaxed.

The butler shuffled his feet, edging toward the door of the study while Jason made a great show of neatening up, taking his time to straighten the various piles of papers, books, and other odds and ends spread across the polished mahogany surface. Then, with a satisfied nod, he settled back down in his chair and reached for the ivory paper knife with one hand and a stack of unopened correspondence with the other. Lord, he had come to a pretty pass when twitting his butler was the brightest spot in his day.

"M-my lord," Gower spluttered. "Perhaps you misunderstood. Your guests have arrived. You cannot mean to—"

"I did not misunderstand, but my stepmother is hardly a guest. She should know her way around after all these years, but if she wants a tour, have the housekeeper—"

"Beg pardon, my lord, but Mrs. Maddoc is occupied just at present."

Jason took the top letter off the pile and slid the edge of his knife under the wax seal. "I, too, am occupied. I have put off responding to, ah—" He glanced down to ascertain the sender. It was from his stepmother. He cursed and set the paper aside, reaching for the next letter. A glance at the handwriting showed it was from the same source. He thumbed through the remainder of the stack before setting it back upon his desk.

Gower shook his head. "Her ladyship is the only person who still bothers to write you. Everyone else has either given up or addressed their concerns to your man of business."

Jason rubbed his temples. This was the problem with having retainers who had known him from the time he was in short coats. They had no compunction about making their displeasure known.

"Do I pay you to be impertinent, Gower?"

"If I may be so bold, my lord, you don't pay me at all. Your dearly departed father left me a generous pension in his will. I've the means to retire if I so choose."

"Are you tendering your resignation, then?" Jason asked flatly, as though the butler's answer meant nothing to him.

"You would be rightly served if I did, and Mrs. Maddoc, too, but neither of us is leaving while there's life in our bodies and Trahernes residing here at Castle Arlyss."

Jason released his breath. "I can't get rid of the servants I don't pay or keep the ones I do," he grumbled. "The maids don't last long enough to learn their way about the house. I swear not a month goes by without Mrs. Maddoc informing me that yet another maidservant has quit her post. That would mean, what, eleven maids have come and gone this year?"

"Twelve. Bess left this morning."

"Bess," Jason repeated, frowning. "Wasn't she was the one who——?"

"She was the only one, my lord."

"The only one who what?"

"The only maid, my lord." Gower's expression was that of a long-suffering parent saddled with an unnecessarily stupid child.

"Don't be ridiculous, Gower. A place this size can't function without maids."

"Quite so, and we're in a fair bind being so short-staffed, but perhaps I should clarify: Bess was the only remaining chambermaid. The under-maids usually aren't scared off, as they never come in contact with, er——" The butler cleared his throat. "In any event, Mrs. Maddoc has placed several advertisements——"

"Scared off?" Jason pushed to his feet and began to pace the room. "Christ, has some ninnyhammer been spreading tales about that bloody ghost again? Or is it the curse on the Traherene brides this time? You know I won't stand for gossip among the servants."

"My lord, your guests are waiting for——"

Jason stopped, fixing his butler with an icy stare. "Answer the question."

"Very well," the butler replied stiffly, drawing himself up to his full height. With his back straight, the man's bushy white eyebrows were in line with Jason's collarbone. "There has been no mention of ghosts or curses, at least in my hearing, since you forbade such talk."

"Then what the devil is scaring these silly chits off?" Jason snapped.

Gower fixed his attention on the study's coffered ceiling. "I couldn't say, I'm sure," he murmured. "Mayhap they're frightened of those demon hounds always trotting along at your heels."

Jason looked over at the two massive Danes sleeping on their backs in front of the fireplace. With their front paws drawn up to their chests, they looked more comical than ferocious. "They wouldn't harm a flea——" He held up a hand as Gower opened his mouth to protest. "——without some provocation. Yes, I remember how they viciously atta— assaulted you. You certainly take every opportunity to remind me. Give over, Gower. You weren't harmed and neither of them has so much as barked in your direction in years."

Jason shot a sideways glance at the dogs he'd rescued years before from a bear-baiting in London. They had recovered from the experience in most respects, but there were certain commands so harshly beaten into them, an eternity wouldn't be long enough to forget.

A familiar anger welled up, its dark currents flowing through his veins, stirring his blood. Being deceived and abandoned by the one most implicitly trusted . . . Such betrayal cut deep. The physical scars had healed and faded, but there were other scars no amount of patience or affection could erase.

"My lord, are you well?"

Jason heard the butler speak as from a great distance. He forced his eyes to focus on the older man's worried visage. "Quite well," he responded, unclenching his fists. "I got lost in the past for a moment."

"If there is anything I can. . . ?" Gower trailed off as Jason shook his head sharply.

"There is nothing anyone can do, short of turning back time."

The butler fiddled with one of the buttons on his austere black coat. "May I suggest you allow yourself to be distracted for a while? Your guests are waiting in the Great Hall——"

"Damnation, didn't you hear me before? I have no wish to play at being the gracious host, and it isn't necessary in this case. My stepmother is not a guest, nor is my half sister."

"The marchioness and Lady Charlotte are family and thus more deserving of your attention. As it happens, however, you do have a guest. There is a young woman come with them."

Jason shrugged. "She's probably Charlotte's nurse."

"I hope your lordship is not suggesting I cannot tell a gentlewoman of good breeding from a maidservant." Gower's tone had more starch than his cravat.

"I wouldn't dare." Jason sighed. "You're not going to leave off until I greet them, are you?"

"No, my lord."

"Very well," Jason grumbled, stalking toward the door. "You're a nuisance, Gower. Remind me later to turn you out without references."

"Of course, my lord," the butler agreed. "The day would feel woefully incomplete were I not dismissed at least once."

Maggie Robinson/Margaret Rowe

Maggie Robinson/Margaret Rowe is a former teacher, library clerk and mother of four who woke up in the middle of the night absolutely compelled to create the perfect man and use as many adverbs as possible doing so. A transplanted New Yorker, she lives with her not-quite perfect husband in Maine, where the cold winters are ideal for staying inside and writing hot historical romances.

Maggie Robinson writes sexy historical romps for Kensington's Brava line; Margaret Rowe writes emotional, edgy Regency noir for Berkley Heat.

You can find out more about Maggie Robinson by visiting http://www.maggierobinson.net, and more about Margaret Rowe at http://www.margaretrowe.net.

Praise for Maggie Robinson

"*Mistress by Mistake* sizzles off the page. A marvelously sexy romp."
- Anna Campbell, award-winning author and RITA® finalist

Praise for Margaret Rowe

"Tempting Eden is a deeply emotional story that offers both wicked heat and delicious connection."
- Victoria Dahl, award-winning author and RITA® finalist

Mistress by Mistake

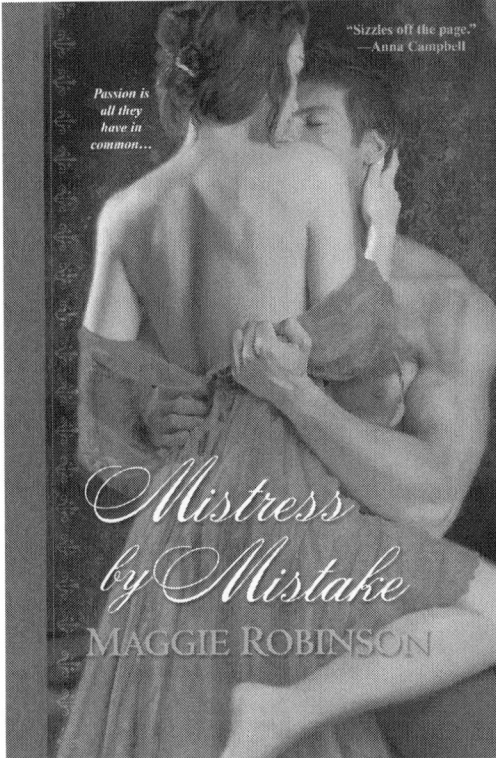

Scandal is only the beginning...

Charlotte Fallon let her guarded virtue fall once—and she's paid dearly for it ever since. She swore she'd never succumb to men's desires again. But even a village spinster's life miles from temptation can't save her from a sister with no shame whatsoever. Or a heart that longs for more, whatever the cost...

Sir Michael Bayard found more than he expected in his bed when he finally joined his new mistress. He'd fantasized about her dewy skin and luscious curves, assured her understanding that what passed between them was mere dalliance. But he didn't expect the innocence and heat of her response in his arms. Nor her surprisingly sharp tongue once she was out of them...

A few days of abandon cannot undo the hard-learned lessons of a lifetime. Nor can an honest passion burn away the restraints of society's judgments. Unless, of course, one believes in nonsense like true love...

Available May 2010, from Kensington Brava
ISBN-10: 0758250991 ✳*ISBN-13: 978-0758250995*

Chapter One

"Honestly, Charlie! You're ruined anyway! What difference does it make?"

Charlotte felt the room spin every time her sister said the words "honestly, Charlie." Honesty had very little to do with Deborah Fallon. She was a mistress of prevarication. She was a mistress, period.

Charlotte Fallon looked at her sister, her beautiful, selfish, stubborn younger sister. The sister she was always trying to save in one manner or another, not that she'd been successful. Charlotte wished she had tossed her letter into the fire without opening it. "I should never have come."

"Nonsense. This is the ideal solution. Arthur wants to *marry* me, Charlie. I'm not getting any younger, you know. And neither are *you*. Surely you cannot stand there all stiff and disapproving and deny me happiness."

No one of importance had ever denied Deborah Fallon anything. One look at her cloud of black hair and mischievous sky blue eyes, her bee-stung lips and spectacular bosom, and they had fallen at her feet. Since the age of sixteen, she had flaunted her assets and traded one rich man for another. Now twenty-six, she was still lovely and in possession of a very tidy fortune, even tidier now due to the recent infusion of money from the coffers of Sir Michael Xavier Bayard. He was expected to arrive in London from his Dorset estate any day now and fall into Deborah Fallon's bed. His own bed, actually. This house, every stick of furniture, every carpet, every lacy curtain belonged to him, as did the woman who was packing a sleek new trunk.

Charlotte Fallon did not belong to anyone. She also had black hair, only it was confined by hairpins and covered by a starched linen cap. Her sky blue eyes were not mischievous at present, but dismayed. Her bee-stung lips were drawn into a frown, and her spectacular bosom heaved in indignation. "You cannot take Sir Michael's money and run off with Arthur Bannister!"

Deborah continued to fold clothes into the trunk. Charlotte took inventory of her sister's impropriety. Wispy, sensuous underthings trimmed with frivolous ribbons and bows. Low-cut silk dresses in every color of the rainbow. Embroidered slippers. Sheer stockings. Velvet jewel bags filled with precious stones.

"I shall leave you some of my wardrobe. And my pearl and sapphire necklace." Deborah sighed with sacrifice. "It's not as though I'm taking *everything*. I thought for a moment to take the paintings, but after consideration I just couldn't do it to the man. He is very fond of his art, even if they're only minor works by obscure painters. And I'll leave him *you*."

"I don't want to be left! You cannot just install me in your bedchamber and expect Sir Michael not to notice!"

"Of course Bay will notice. He's a very noticing kind of fellow. Those eyes! So black and knowing. They quite gave me shivers. But you and I much alike, or would be if you didn't look like such a prude. Honestly, Charlie, where is the harm? He's a wonderful lover, and lord knows you could do with a bit of amusement."

Charlotte felt a wave of revulsion. "You—you've slept with him already?"

Deborah tossed her black curls. "Don't be absurd. I never let him touch me. Not even a kiss. That's why he paid so much. I was absolutely unattainable without his contract. But," she said, closing the trunk latch with finality, "I'm on good terms with Helena Colbert, my predecessor. It was she who decorated this bedroom." Deborah looked around at the grotesquely chubby cupids that lurked on every surface. "Granted, she does not have much imagination, but she assured me bedding Bay was not a hardship. She said he's quite masterful."

"If that is true, why have you chosen Arthur?" Charlotte had met Arthur Bannister. Charlotte doubted Arthur could master anyone, let alone Deborah. He was the prematurely balding third son of an earl, obviously not destined for the clergy if he married her sister the famous courtesan.

"Arthur is very sweet. He loves me. His family will come round in time." Deborah gave her an assured smile. Everybody *always* loved her; it was inconceivable to her that one could not.

"You don't love *him*, do you." Charlotte did not tack a question mark to her words.

"Honestly, Charlie! What is love anyway? You thought you were in love and look how that turned out. You're thirty years old and live in the country with *cats*." Deborah pulled on her gloves. Pale yellow kidskin. How ridiculous for traveling, but they matched her slippers and flimsy striped dress. Charlotte envisioned her sister discarding the whole outfit in the carriage on the way to Dover just to ensure Arthur continued the journey. "We haven't much time. Thank goodness Bay's grandmother got sick and died and he was called away."

Only Deborah could say such a thing and look like an angel doing it. Charlotte wanted to throttle her sister's slender white neck. "You are attempting to perpetrate fraud, Deb. Theft. For all I know the man will lock me up in prison in your place before he finds you."

"Pooh. He's quite besotted with me. And even if he doesn't like you, you can explain this whole affair far better than I can in a letter. I should be quite thoughtless if I just left a note on the pillow."

An understatement. Deborah had always been thoughtless. She had broken her late parents' hearts when she ran off to London with George, although they did manage to spend the money she sent home at irregular intervals. Charlotte was ashamed to acknowledge that without Deb's help, her cats might go hungry. Of course, the cats weren't really her own. The half-dozen or so were ferociously feral and only visited her out of habit, not gratitude. They would not dream of curling up on the hearth or resting upon her bed pillow or being helpful mousers. No, they yowled for their scraps and milk at the cottage kitchen door when hunting was poor or the weather problematic. They would be perfectly fine until she returned to Little Hyssop after she put her sister's ridiculous scheme behind her.

Deborah patted the feather bed. "Come. Sit down. I have many instructions to give you."

Charlotte blushed as brightly as a virgin, although she could not claim the title. Surely her sister was not going to subject her to courtesan lessons. She was most certainly not going to take Deborah's place in anything but conversation with Sir Michael, who was at least owed an explanation once he returned to Town.

Charlotte reflected it had ever been thus—Deborah would do something impetuous and Charlotte would pick up the pieces. She dearly hoped that Deborah's new protector was not too badly smitten, for she was not good at mending heartbreak, especially her own. She listened with half an ear as Deborah recited a litany of practicalities and positions. Charlotte felt the beginnings of one of her vexing headaches. Any amount of time spent with her little sister was sure to produce such a result. She was never more relieved when Irene, the young maid hired by Sir Michael to attend to whichever mistress was in residence, announced that Mr. Bannister was below and his driver on his way up for the luggage.

Charlotte was tugged downstairs and reintroduced to Arthur, who was a few years Deborah's junior despite the hair loss and beginnings of a paunch. These shortcomings were more than mitigated by the recent death of his great-uncle, who had remembered young Arthur kindly in his will. A pity that the old man had died after Deborah had come to her arrangement with Sir Michael Xavier Bayard. But then illness and another fortuitous death occurred, keeping the baronet in Dorset these past six weeks. Charlotte was afraid that Arthur Bannister had already slept beneath Sir Michael's sheets and could not like him for it.

"Come, my love. The carriage awaits and I've a special license." Arthur patted his breast pocket smugly. Deborah said he'd spared no expense to make London's fairest Cyprian his own. By the time Sir Michael came home, she would be Mrs. Bannister. Of course, they were to travel on the Continent first, just to give his family and Sir Michael a while to calm down. Then Deborah would be a mistress of only Arthur's late uncle's estate in Kent.

Deborah kissed her sister good-bye, and to her horror, Charlotte discovered her eyes were filling with tears. Truly, she wished her sister happy. If she thought for a moment that Arthur Bannister could control Deborah's dishonorable impulses, she might feel very differently about this hasty wedding. Deborah might make a poor wife, but at least one of the Fallon girls would be a bride at last.

Deborah left in a flurry of swishing skirts and lavender water. Suddenly the little house was quiet as a tomb. Somewhere below Irene and Mrs. Kelly, the cook-housekeeper, were engaged in dinner preparations for her. Charlotte didn't think she could eat a bite. A glass of sherry, on the other hand, would steady her nerves for the task ahead. She poured a healthy tot from a crystal decanter and drank it down in one gulp.

To think that her sister wanted her to become a harlot! As if she were at all suited to the position Deborah had cut out for herself almost a decade ago. To foist her on a stranger, to leave Charlotte holding the proverbial bag when Sir Michael returned made her heart skip erratically. She should have known to read between the lines of Deb's badly spelled letter. Anything Deb considered to be an emergency was really a catastrophe.

Charlotte poured another drink. It would not do to get foxed. It was a family curse. Both the Fallon parents had drowned their financial sorrows in a bottle, then drowned in reality when they had the drunken idea to go for one last midnight sail before their beloved boat was repossessed. Charlotte had disposed of their crumbling manor house, paid off their debts and moved as far inland as she could. She had been scrupulous about sharing the pitiful proceeds with her sister. Judging from the contents stuffed in her trunk and stored in the country, Deborah had never needed a farthing. Her gentlemen had been generous from the start.

Charlotte sighed. Her sister had not been so very indiscriminate. She'd had only four lovers in ten years, each of whom had showered her with jewels, money and clothing. Deb had not been able to wheedle anyone out of a house yet—save for poor Arthur. Charlotte should turn tail and go right back home. A note on the pillow would do as well as any stuttering excuse she could give Sir Michael for her sister's behavior.

She returned to Deb's bedroom to regroup, shoving a plaster cupid away to set her drink by the bedside. Lord, but she was tired. The flying trip to town when she imagined her sister dying—or worse! —had sapped every bit of strength she had. And then to discover what Deborah planned—well, it quite took one's breath away.

She lay in the cupid-infested room, nervously bunching the scarlet satin coverlet between her fingers. She would not unpack her own trunk but to pull out her tattered nightrail and robe later. She could not move in and assume her sister's life. She didn't even want to consume her dinner. But an hour later, fresh-faced Irene was at the door informing her that supper was on the table. Charlotte imagined it tasted delicious, but was too distracted to tell. Despite her earlier pledge, she gulped a great deal of wine in order that she might actually fall asleep in her sister's bed. Woozy and warm, she allowed Irene to help her undress and bathe, then crawled under the covers, closing her eyes to the grinning statues. How Deborah had born them for six weeks was a wonder.

She slept as if dead, having the most delightful tipsy dream somewhere past midnight. But when morning came and she found her nightgown hanging from a fat angel's head and a naked man with his lips planted firmly around her left nipple, she knew her dream was now a nightmare.

Mistress by Midnight

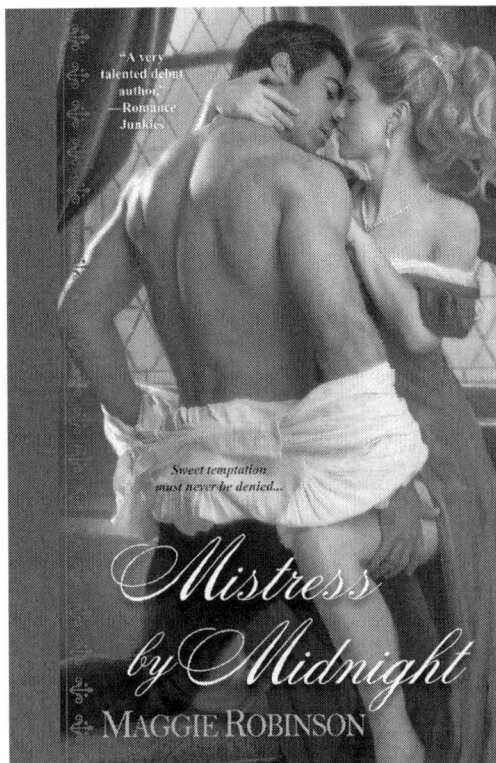

Nothing can break their bond, not even their desperate midnight bargain....

As children, Desmond Ryland, Marquess of Conover, and Laurette Vincent were inseparable. As young adults, their friendship blossomed into love. But then fate intervened, sending them down different paths. Years later, Con still can't forget his beautiful Laurette. Now he's determined to make her his forever. There's just one problem. Laurette keeps refusing his marriage proposals. Throwing honor to the wind, Con decides that the only way Laurette will wed him is if he thoroughly seduces her...

Laurette's pulse still quickens every time she thinks of Con and the scorching passion they once shared. She aches to taste the pleasure Con offers her. But she knows she can't. For so much has happened since they were last lovers. But how long can she resist the consuming desire that demands to be obeyed?

Available January 2011, from Kensington Brava
ISBN-10: 0758251017 ✳ISBN-13: 978-0758251015

Prologue

Despite it being high summer, Con was so pale he looked ill. But he had come to her at the ring of stones, and that was the important thing.

In a few days time, he would belong to some other woman. He would stand in front of the altar at All Saints and pledge his troth to Marianna Berryman, that sleek stranger who looked very like a cream-fed cat.

Laurette understood this intellectually. It was something he had to do for the sake of his estate and all the people who depended on him. There were two villages in his purview which had suffered year after year from neglect. The prosperity of the local populace rested upon the shoulders of a nineteen year old boy. When others his age were out carousing, he was promising his future away.

What she planned for the twilight was foolish. It would mean nothing in the wider world, but it meant everything to her. She smoothed the fabric of her beaded blue dress—the dress she had worn for her hopeless come-out—and almost enjoyed the shock on Con's face when he saw her. She had lowered the neckline—if her chest were the heavens, infinite constellations of stars were twinkling brightly.

But Con loved her freckles.

"I am considerably underdressed, I see." He wore a homespun shirt and breeches, clean but worn. New clothes were filling his closets, but she was glad he didn't come to her wearing Berryman largesse.

"This is a special occasion."

Con laughed a bit bleakly. "Yes, it's Wednesday evening. Bring out the fireworks."

"I didn't think of those. But I do have a bottle of champagne I pinched from my father's cellar."

"I'm not thirsty, Laurie." He collapsed onto the ground, but made no motion for her to join him. She could feel his retreat as though it were a living thing. Carefully she spread her skirts and sat beside him.

"You'll ruin that dress."

She shrugged. "I'll never wear it again. But I wanted to wear it for you tonight. So you would remember."

"I'll never forget you, Laurie, and that's the problem."

She grabbed a hand. "It's to be my wedding dress, Con. I'm going to marry you tonight."

He pulled away. "Don't be daft. I've signed all the papers. Berryman will send me to jail if I renege now."

"You'll marry on Saturday, just as they planned. But your heart will always belong to me."

"You know it will, but what good is even saying it? This is over, Laurie. *We* are over."

His words were brutal. He looked angry, his thick black brows drawn into a frown.

"Please give me tonight, Con. I want us to stand in this magical place under God's sky. To speak what's in my heart. To be your wife of the heart, if not in a church register."

She searched his face for a reaction. At first there was none. Then residual anger turned to incredulity, and, eventually, a faint smile.

"A pagan wedding for my pagan girl. It's not much to cling to."

"It's all I'll ever have," she said simply.

He kissed her then, too gently. She stole control and pushed him on his back, eating him up as if she were starving. If she didn't stop she would make love to him before she said the words she had labored over so long. She broke the kiss, leaping to her feet.

"We shall continue all that in a moment, my Lord Conover. First I want you to stand up with me before the altar stone."

He shook his head. "You really are serious."

"I am."

"All right." Con got to his feet, brushing off his threadbare pants. "I wish—"

Laurette placed a finger on his lips. "No regrets. We have tonight, as the sun is sinking and the shadows loom. Now, hold my hands."

"Yes, madam." He brought them to his lips.

"That's soon to be Lady Conover to you. Oh, don't look so stricken. I know this is all pretense. But when winter comes, the thought of this summer evening will keep me warm."

"It's not enough."

"It will have to be. Now then." She squeezed his hands. "I, Laurette Isabella Vincent, do take thee, Desmond—"

"Thee?"

"Quiet. Your turn will come. Do take thee, Desmond Anthony Ryland, seventh Marquess of Conover, to be the husband of my heart and keeper of my soul and body for all eternity. Though circumstances may part us, nothing will ever break the bonds of our friendship and love."

The next part was tricky. She certainly was not going to promise to *obey*. Not Con or anyone.

"I do solemnly promise to be mindful of thy wishes in all things, even if I do not always agree. I will love you—*thee*—and support thee until I cease to draw breath. I pledge this to thee before the altar of the Ancients, in the sight of God our Father, whose ways may be a mystery at present."

There had been more, but her throat was becoming thick as Con looked down on her, his black eyes somber. "Amen."

He kissed the tear from her cheek. "I, Desmond Anthony Ryland, seventh Marquess of Conover, take thee Laurette Isabella Vincent as my wedded wife of the heart. I shall be true to thee until death. I love you so much, Laurie, my heart is breaking."

They held each other as the sun dipped behind the megalith, casting its last light on the sparkles of Laurette's dress. The champagne was forgotten, but the consummation of their union was not.

Chapter One

LONDON, 1820

Laurette knew precisely what she must do. Again. Had known even before her baby brother had fallen so firmly into the Marquess of Conover's clutches.

To be fair, perhaps Charlie had not so much fallen as thrown himself headfirst into Con's way. Charlie had been as heedless as she herself had been more than a decade ago. She was not immune even now to Con's inconvenient presence. She had shown him her back on more than one occasion, but could feel the heat of his piercing black gaze straight through to her tattered stays.

But tonight she would allow him to look his fill, going so far as having visited Madame Demarche this afternoon for her naughtiest underpinnings. Laurette would have one less thing for which to feel shame.

Purchased with credit, of course. One more bill to join the mountain of debt. Insurmountable as a Himalayan peak and just as chilling. Nearly as cold as Conover's heart.

She raised the lion's head knocker and let it fall, once, composing herself to face Con's servant.

Desmond Ryland, Marquess of Conover, opened the door himself.

"You!"

"Did you think I would allow you to be seen here at such an hour?" he asked, his face betraying no emotion. "You must indeed think me a veritable devil. I've sent Aram to bed. Come into my study."

He *was* a devil, suggesting this absurd time. Midnight, as though they were two foreign spies about to exchange vital information in utmost secrecy.

Laurette followed him down the shadowy hall, the black and white tile a chessboard beneath her feet. She felt much like a pawn, but would soon need to become the White Queen. Con must not know just how desperate she was.

Though he surely must suspect.

He opened a door and stepped aside as she crossed the threshold. The room, she knew, was his sanctuary, filled with objects he'd collected in the years he'd been absent from Town and her life. Absent from his own life, as well. The marquessate had been shockingly abandoned for too long.

She had been summoned here once before, in daylight, a year ago. She was better prepared tonight. She allowed her filmy shawl to slip from one shoulder but refused Con's offer of a chair.

"Suit yourself," he shrugged, sitting behind his desk. He placed a hand on a decanter of brandy. "Will you join me? We can toast to old times."

Laurette shook her head. She's need every shred of her wits to get through what was ahead. "No thank you, my lord."

She could feel the thread of attraction between them, frayed yet stubborn. She should be too old and wise now to view anything that was to come as more than a business arrangement. As soon as she had seen the bold strokes of his note, she had accepted its implication. She was nearly thirty, almost half her life away from when Conover first beguiled her. Or perhaps when she had beguiled him. He had left her long ago, but not quite soon enough.

A pop from the fire startled her, and she turned to watch sparks fly onto the marble tiles. The room was uncomfortably warm for this time of year, but it was said that the Marquess of Conover had learned to love the heat of the exotic East on his travels.

"I appeal to your goodness," Laurette said, nearly choking on her words' improbability.

"I find good men dead boring, my dear. Good women, too." Con abandoned his desk and strode across the floor, where she was rooted by feet that suddenly felt too heavy to lift. He smiled, looking almost boyish, and fingered the single loose golden curl teasing the ivory slope of her shoulder. She recalled he had always been dazzled by her hair and imagined just this touch when she had tugged the strand down.

She had hoped to appear winsome despite the passage of time, but her plan was working far too well for current comfort. She pushed him away with more force than she felt. "What would you know about good men, my lord?" She scraped the offending hair back with trembling fingers under the prison of its hairpin. It wouldn't do to tempt him further. Or herself. What had she been thinking to come here?

"I've known my share. But I am uncertain if your brother fits the category. A good, earnest young fellow, on occasion. A divinity student, is he not? But then—I fear his present vices make him ill-suited for his chosen profession. Among other things, he is so dishonorable he sends his sister in his stead. Your letter was quite affecting. You've gone to a great deal of trouble on his account, but I hardly see why I should forgive his debt." He folded his arms and leaned forward. "Convince me."

Damn him. He intended her to beg. They both knew how it would end.

"He does not know I'm here. He knows nothing," Laurette said quickly, stepping backward.

He was upon her again, his warm brandied breath sending shivers down her spine. She toppled backward onto a leather chair. A small mercy. At least she wouldn't fall foolishly at his feet. She closed her eyes, remembering herself in such a pose, Con's head thrown back, his fingers entwined in the tangle of her hair. A lifetime ago.

She looked up. His cheek was creased in amusement at her clumsiness. "He will not thank you for your interference."

"I'm not interfering! He is much too young to fall prey to your evil machinations."

Con raised a black winged brow. "Such melodramatic vocabulary. He's not that young, you know. Much older than you were when you were so very sure of yourself. And by calling me evil you defeat your purpose, Laurette. Why, I might take offense and not cooperate. Perhaps I *am* a very good man to discourage him from gambling he can ill afford. But I *will* be repaid. " He leaned over, placing his hands on the arms of Laurette's chair. His eyes were dark, obsidian, but his intentions clear.

Laurette felt her blush rise and leaned back against her seat. She willed herself to stay calm. He would not crowd her and make her cower beneath him. She raised her chin a fraction. "He cannot—that is to say, our funds are tied up at present. Our guardian..." She trailed off, never much able to lie well. But she was expert at keeping secrets.

Con left her abruptly to return to his desk. She watched as he poured himself another brandy into the crystal tumbler, but let it sit untouched. "What do you propose, Laurette?" he asked, his voice a velvet burr. "That I tear up your brother's vowels and give him the cut direct next time we meet?"

"Yes," Laurette said boldly. "The sum he owes must be a mere trifle to you. And his company a bore. If you hurt his feelings now, it will only be to his ultimate benefit. One day he will see that." She glanced around Lord Conover's study, appointed with elegance and treasure. Brass fittings gleamed in the candlelight. A thick Persian carpet lay under her scuffed kid slippers. The study was the lair of a man of exquisite taste, a far cry from Charlie's disreputable lodging. She twisted her fingers, awaiting his next words.

There was the faintest trace of a smile. "You give me far too much credit. I am neither a good man, nor, despite what you see here, so rich man a man I can ignore a debt this size. We all need blunt to keep up appearances. And settle obligations."

Laurette knew exactly to the penny what his obligation to her cost him and held her tongue.

Con leaned back in his chair, the picture of confidence. "If I cannot have coin, some substitution must be made. I think you know what will please me."

Laurette nodded. It would please her too, God forgive her. Her voice didn't waver. "When, Con?"

He picked up his glass and drained it. "Tonight. I confess I cannot wait to have you in my bed again."

Laurette searched her memory. There had been very few beds involved in their brief affair. Making love to Con in one would be a luxurious novelty. She was not prepared, however; the vial of sponges was still secreted away in her small trunk at her brother's rooms. She had not allowed herself to think the evening would end in quite this way. But she had just finished her courses. Surely she was safe.

"Very well." She rose from the haven of her chair.

His face showed the surprise he surely felt. Good. It was time she unsettled *him*.

"You seem to be taking your fate rather calmly, Laurette."

"Did you arrange it? That it would come to this?" she asked softly.

"Did I engage your brother in a high stakes game he had no hope of winning? I declare, that avenue had not occurred to me," Con said smoothly. "How you must despise me to even ask." He motioned her to him. After a few awkward moments, Laurette walked toward him and allowed him to pull her down into his lap. He was undeniably hard, fully aroused. She let herself feel a brief surge of triumph.

He placed a broad hand across her abdomen and settled her even closer. "How is the child?"

Was this an unconscious gesture? Con had never felt her daughter where his hand now lay, had never seen her, held her. She fought the urge to slap his hand away and willed herself to melt into the contours of his hard body. It would go quicker if she just gave in and let him think he'd won. "Very well, my lord. How is yours?"

"Fast asleep in his dormitory, I hope, surrounded by other scruffy little villains. I should like you to meet him one day."

She did not tell him that his son was already known to her, as his wife had once been, improbably, her friend. "I don't believe that would be wise, my lord."

"Why not? If you recall, I offered you the position as his step-mama a year ago. It is past time you become acquainted with my son, and I your daughter." His busy fingers had begun removing hairpins.

Laurette said nothing, lulling in his arms as his lips skimmed her throat, his hands stroking every exposed inch. In dressing tonight, she'd bared as much of her flesh as she dared in order to tempt him. She wondered how she could so deceive herself. Nothing had changed. Nothing would ever change. And that was the problem.

Laurette pressed a gloved finger to his lips. "We do not need to discuss the past, my lord. We have tonight."

"If you think," he growled, "that I will be satisfied with only one night with you, you're as mad as ever."

An insult. Lucky that, for she suddenly retrieved her primness and relative virtue. She straightened up. "That is all I am willing to offer."

He stood in anger, dumping her unceremoniously into his chair. "My dear Miss Vincent, if you wish me to forgive your brother's debts—all of them—I require a bit more effort on your part."

"A-all? What do you mean?"

"I see the young fool didn't tell you." Con pulled open a drawer, fisting a raft of crumpled paper. "Here. Read them and then tell me one paltry night with you is worth ten thousand pounds. Even you cannot have such a high opinion of yourself."

Laurette's felt her tongue thicken and lips go numb. "It cannot be," she whispered.

"I've spent the past month buying up his notes all over town." Con's smile, feral and harsh, withered her even further. He now followed in his father-in-law's footsteps.

"You did this."

"You may think what you wish. I hold the mortgage to Vincent Lodge as well. You've denied me long enough, Laurie."

Her home, ramshackle as it was. Beatrix's home, if only on brief holidays away from her foster family. Laurette had forgotten just how stubborn and high-handed Conover could be. She looked at him, hoping to appear as haughty as the queen she most certainly was not.

"What kind of man are you?"

"Not a *good* one, I wager. I offered you my name once. I shan't do so again. Your refusal still rings in my ears. But I need a mistress. You once played the part to perfection. The position is yours if you want it."

Laurette considered. She could do it, but he would pay—far more than the price of her brother's losses.

She scooped up her hairpins from her skirt. "All right. The notes, if you please."

Con locked them into the desk drawer and pocketed the key. "Very amusing. You'd toss them into the fire and laugh all the way home. No, my dear. We are going upstairs. Now. As a show of good faith. The vouchers will be destroyed once I engage your services in a binding agreement. A year, I should think, will suit me."

Laurette's lips twisted in distaste. How had she ever thought to get around this man? She was as much an innocent as before. "But it will not suit me."

"Still full of misplaced pride, I see." Con ran a long finger down her cheek and she felt herself flush. "Six months, then. Surely you can endure my lovemaking for that amount of time."

"I shall endeavor to do so." He might own her body, but never her heart. Not again. Six months would seem an eternity. "What of Charlie?"

"He's about to go on a Grand Tour. A trip to the Holy Land is in order, with a tutor, far from the gaming tables and whores. Yes," he added, as she stiffened beneath his fingers, "your brother has devoutly been studying all manner of carnal pleasures. I spoke with him this afternoon. He's actually most eager to get away."

She shivered. "Does he know what you plan for me? For us?"

Con raised another irritated eyebrow. "Come now. Give me points for discretion. I know how to be a marquess now. I'm not still some love-struck boy. I've kept my tongue this time." He cupped her cheek, almost tenderly. "It's all arranged, Laurie. A little house on Jane Street, not far from here. You may even have the child visit if you desire."

"Beatrix. Her name is Beatrix," Laurette whispered.

Con pulled her to him, kissing her forehead. "I know her name. I am her father, after all."

Mistress by Marriage

Seducing one's own wife has never been so satisfying...

Lady Caroline Christie has felt the chill of society's disapproval all her life—never more so than during her marriage to 'Cold Christie.' What's one more scandal when her husband proposes to divorce her?

Baron Edward Christie finds Caroline impossible—to live with, or forget. But when he decides to end their tumultuous marriage for all the right reasons, he discovers his heart has a reason of its own.

Available September 2011, from Kensington Brava

Prologue

Edward Christie had been an utter fool six years ago. True, he'd had plenty of company. Every man in the room had gaped when Caroline Parker entered Lady Huntington's ballroom. Conversation stilled. Hearts hammered. Shoulders straightened. Chests and areas lower swelled.

There were many reasons for these changes. There was her hair, of course, masses of it, red as lava and swirled up with diamonds. Diamond earrings and a diamond necklace and diamond bracelets were festooned all over her creamy skin, too, skin so delicious every man whose tongue was hanging out longed to lap it. Her eyes were liquid silver, bright as stars and fringed with midnight black lashes, so at odds with her hair. And her dress—a shocking scarlet for an unmarried woman—for *any* woman—had a diamond brooch hovering over the most spectacular assets he'd ever seen. The jewels were all paste, as he was later to find out, but her breasts were very real.

There were known drawbacks, which quickly circulated about the room, prodded along by spiteful cats who were quite eclipsed by Caroline's magnificence. She was old, at least twenty-five, and her family—what there was of it—was dirt poor and touched by scandal. Some said her brother died in a duel; others said he was killed by one of his many mistresses. She had a sister in Canada, living in some godforsaken outpost in the snow with her lieutenant husband and howling wolves. Her parents were long dead and she was clinging to the ton by the weakest of threads; the distant cousin who inherited her brother's title was anxious to get her off his hands before he put his hands all over her and irritated his irritable wife.

Edward had obliged in a courtship of less than five days. Baron Christie had spent his first thirty-four years never, ever being at all impulsive, and his sudden marriage by special license to a woman who looked like an expensive courtesan was the *on dit* of the season. He had buried one wife, the perfectly staid and proper Alice, whose brown hair would never be compared to living fire and whose brown eyes could only be compared to mud. Alice, who'd quickly and quietly done her duty and provided him with an heir, a spare and a little girl who looked just as angular and forbidding as her father. Alice, who'd caught a chill one week and died the next and was no doubt rolling over in her grave to be supplanted by Caroline Parker.

Edward had no one to blame but himself. He didn't need more children, and Caroline hadn't any money. But what she did have—what she *was*—had upended Edward's life for one hellish year before he came to his senses and put her away.

Caroline had no one to blame but herself. It was her pride, her dreadful Parker pride, which had prevented her from saying one simple word—no. If only her rosy lips had opened and she had managed to get her tongue to the roof of her mouth and expelled sufficient air, she would not have found herself living in Jane Street, home to the most notorious courtesans in London.

When Edward asked her to marry him after less than a week's acquaintance, she should have said no. When he'd asked her that horrible, vile, *impertinent* question five years ago, she should have said no. But instead she'd said yes to the first question, rather gratefully if truth be told, and hadn't said a word to the second, just cast her husband the most scornful look she could conjure up and showed him her back.

Caroline was no man's mistress, despite her exclusive Jane Street address and rumors to the contrary. In the five years since she and her husband separated, he had come to her door but once a year, the anniversary of the night she was unable to utter that one-syllable word. They took ruthless pleasure in each other, and then Edward would disappear again. She, however, remained, ostracized from polite society, completely celibate and despite her ardent hopes, a mother to only the curious contingent of young women who shared her street. The children changed, but the game remained the same. From experienced opera dancers to fresh-faced country girls who had been led astray by rich gentlemen, Caroline watched the parade of mistresses come and go. She passed teacups and handkerchiefs and advice, feeling much older than her almost thirty-one years.

But when she looked in her pier glass, she was still relatively youthful, her red curls shiny, her gray eyes bright. She might have been stouter than she wished, but the prideful Parkers were known to run to fat in middle age. For some reason Edward had let her keep some of the lesser Christie jewels, so there was always a sparkle on her person even if there was no spark to her life. She made the best of it, however, and had some surprising success recently writing wicked novels that she couldn't seem to write fast enough. Her avocation would have stunned her old governess, as Caroline had showed no aptitude whatsoever for grammar lessons or spelling as a girl. Fortunately, her publisher was grammatical and spelled accurately enough for both of them. Her *Courtesan Court* series was highly popular with both society members and their servants alike. There were happy endings galore for the innocent girls led astray, and the wicked always got what was coming to them. She modeled nearly every villain on Edward. It was most satisfactory to shoot him or toss him off a cliff in the final pages. Once she crushed him in a mining mishap, his elegant sinewy body and dark head entombed for all eternity with coal that was as black as his heart.

Of course, sometimes her heroes were modeled on him, too—men with pride nearly as perverse as the Parkers, facile fingers who knew *just* where to touch a girl, and particularly long, thick, entirely perfect penises. Caroline missed Edward's penis, although she didn't miss his conversation much. He was so damned proper and critical, and had been beyond boring to live with. Controlled. Controlling. Humorless. Once he'd installed her as his baroness, it was as if he woke up horrified at what he'd actually done. Whom he'd actually married. It was no wonder she—

No, she couldn't blame him. She had no one to blame but herself.

Tempting Eden

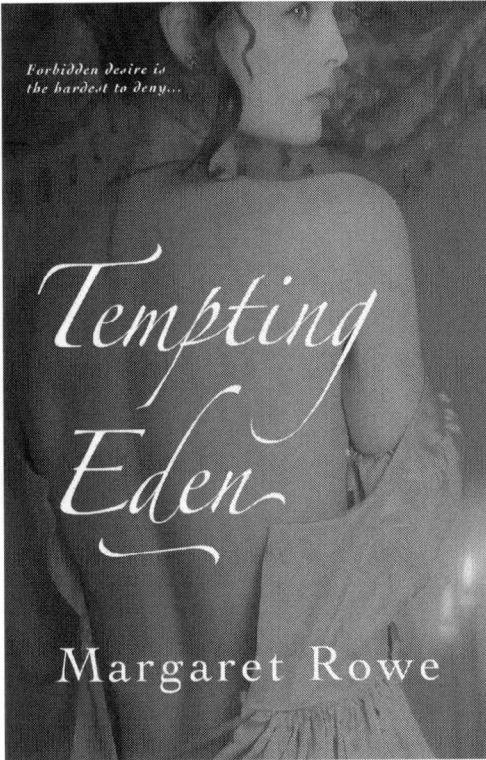

Forbidden desire is the hardest to deny...

The perfect gentleman, and the imperfect woman who makes him forget all his good intentions...

Eden Emery is no stranger to sin. To keep her sister safe from harm, she's paid a steep price with her body—and very nearly lost her soul. But when Baron Ivor Hartford, the very Devil himself finally dies, her troubles are far from over.

Major Stuart Hartford, the late baron's nephew, is in the market for an honorable wife, but first he has to take care of the matter of his Uncle Ivor's ward—a young woman who makes him question the virtue of being proper. For the passion she incites burns away his inhibitions and inflames his heart.

But Eden has vowed to never again cede her destiny to a man. And Hart is left with no choice but to tempt the temptress herself, to show the woman he longs to possess forever that passion can heal, that the sins of the past can be overcome, and that submission can be the greatest power of all.

Available June 2010, from Berkley Heat
ISBN-10: 0425234312 ✴ISBN-13: 978-0425234310

Prologue

When he was done, she'd be the greatest whore in all Christendom.

If they'd been in London, her body would have already been sold to the highest bidder in the Marriage Mart. He'd have to dower her for some chinless earl to take his pleasure in her innocence. Since London was out of the question, a *ton* marriage not on her horizon, there was no better man than he to teach her. She was destined to be a prim little prude if he didn't intervene.

And she might prove more capable than her mother in providing him with an heir. No one would dare question him and live to tell the tale.

Baron Ivor Hartford watched his stepdaughter Eden carefully as she sat across the gleaming mahogany dining table. He'd planted the seeds patiently, and soon it would be time for the harvest.

Her pale plain face was flushed. She giggled.

Excellent.

She was not usually a giggler, but a serious girl. Earnest. Clutching her dead father's dusty books to her ripening bosom with fervor, she had long surpassed the learning of the governess who was abovestairs with his younger stepdaughter. But Ivor would soon further Eden's education beyond her wildest imaginings.

Now he saw her attempt to rise from the table and sway. The footman rushed to catch her.

"I'll take care of her, Henley," the baron said.

All night he had signaled Henley to refill Eden's glass. They had been quite alone at dinner. His wife was upstairs recovering from yet another miscarriage, deep in her laudanum dreams.

When Eden had placed her hand unsteadily over her wine goblet, Ivor had teased her. "Why, puss, you're a grown woman now. Eighteen. If you were in Town, you'd be drinking champagne and whirling about the dance floor with the young bucks. You might even be married and a mother yourself. A little wine won't hurt you."

He had cajoled and flattered, and she had drunk.

He picked her up now and carried her up the stairs. He sent her maid Mattie away to fetch some headache powder. No doubt Eden would have need of it.

Hartford placed her on her bed. Her arms were still around his neck. He disentangled her, brushing against her breasts, then settling his hands firmly on each luscious mound. Her eyes flew open in surprise.

"So beautiful, puss," he whispered. "You've bewitched me. I cannot help myself." Then he bent to kiss her full on the mouth. As her lips opened in protest, his tongue took advantage.

"Mm. You taste like spring wine. Delicious. Sleep well, puss, and dream of me."

Chapter One

Eden Emery was well and truly ruined. In all senses of the word.

She didn't resemble the sort of female that one would even *want* to ruin. She was as thin as a wraith, having lost her appetite for food and most other things quite some time ago. Her tightly braided schoolgirl plaits, shadowed gray eyes and pale skin made her unexceptional, perhaps even unappealing, in every way. But one man had not thought so, and he lay dead in her bed.

Somewhere down the long hallway her sister Jannah coughed. Eden couldn't turn to her for help. Jannah would expire from shock knowing the lengths that Eden had gone to keep her safe. Warm. Fed. Untouched.

Eden turned away from Ivor Hartford's body and washed herself thoroughly, scrubbing the sin from her skin with an almost vicious vigor. Her own body now repelled her because it had so compelled him. Her mother had not been in her grave a day before the man had come back to her bed. He'd ridden her hard to prove his dominance, and she had let him, as she let him do everything.

He had trained her well. He'd said and done things to her to weave her into his web, as helpless and mindless as a fly. She had even betrayed her own mother without much remorse when the woman was alive. How foolish Eden had been, thinking the baron might leave her alone once there was no one to trick.

What a selfish, naïve idiot Eden had been. Jealous, at the heart of it. She had a beautiful, stupid mother, and she was an ugly, smart daughter. She'd been every bit as stupid as her poor mother. More so.

How simple it was to fall into their old routine once her mother was gone.

With one flick of an eye or raised eyebrow, Eden knew what was expected of her, and knew the consequences if she refused.

Not that she would think to do so.

At least Ivor was a man of habit. After he had established his unquestionable mastery over her once again, he slept in her bedchamber Saturday nights, the better to torture her in church Sunday morning with his pious façade, and spent Sunday evenings celebrating his own peculiar brand of religion. Occasionally he varied from this routine, just to keep Eden sufficiently off-kilter. In fact, tonight was Wednesday.

She dressed herself in her most severe black woolen gown, a leftover of what seemed like endless years of mourning, twisting her braids into an unbecoming bun, neutralizing her womanhood with studied care. Holding her breath, she cleaned her stepfather as best she could and struggled to get him back into his dressing gown. She no longer had the need to keep her tongue and told him in plain and vulgar language how he had robbed her of her future, even if in her long-ago childish vanity she had been more than complicit. She spoke of her late father, a surprisingly ecumenical country vicar, who'd named his children for the paradise of different cultures.

Elysium, her beloved brother Eli, had died at Waterloo. Jannah was dying down the hall. Eden herself had shrunk in size as she grew in sin. There had been no heaven on earth for any of Vicar Emery's offspring. However, there was no doubt in her mind that Lord Hartford was going to Hell, no matter what it was called. And she would soon follow.

When Eden was satisfied that every button was buttoned and all traces of his wicked pleasure were gone, she straightened Ivor's body on the bed and rolled him off, where he landed with an unpleasant thud. She stripped the bed and stuffed the soiled sheets in her wardrobe, then smoothed the coverlet over the bare mattress. The room needed airing as well. Shivering, she opened both windows into the night. The candles flared. Lord Hartford had always insisted on light, the better to see her humiliation and ultimate compliance. And sometimes, he used the candles for altogether different purposes.

She arranged an open book on the floor near her chair, neatly placing her magnifying glass on the side table. She then sat down and counted to one hundred, listening to her heart race, composing her thoughts. Should she ring for the servants? No, that implied she was in control of her emotions. And she certainly was not that. She wondered if they could be trusted to keep the manner and location of Lord Hartford's death quiet. He had used them with as little charity as he did his stepdaughter. Rising, she closed the windows and flew out into the hall.

Any Wicked Thing

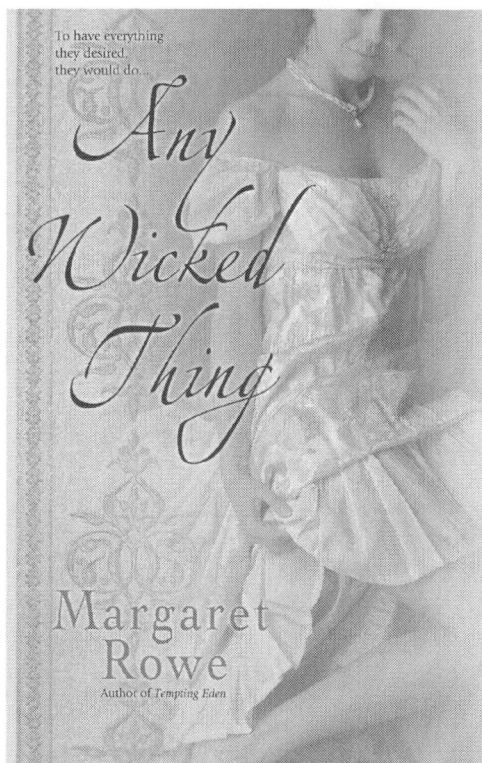

To have everything they desired, they would do any wicked thing...

Ten years ago, Sebastian Goddard, heir to the duchy of Roxbury, was trapped in his father's decaying Yorkshire castle and almost trapped into marriage. How was he to know that the luscious masked milkmaid who seduced him as he counted the stars from a roofless tower was his pesky childhood friend Frederica Wells?

After a decade of decadence, Sebastian returns to find Freddie all grown up and more appealing than ever. But will she still want him when she learns Sebastian's secret sins?

Available Winter 2011, from Berkley Heat
ISBN-10: 0425238644 ✳*ISBN-13: 978-0425238646*

Chapter One

He has not changed a bit. Except to become more handsome. ~~I hate~~
~~him.~~
—From the diary of Frederica Wells

YORKSHIRE, JUNE 1808

"What is the point?" Sebastian Goddard, reluctant heir to the duchy of
Roxbury, looked around the Long Gallery with disfavor after a particularly
adept *attacque du fer*. Grim and grimy portraits of gentlemen who thankfully
were not his ancestors glared down from the castle walls. Motes of dust swirled
in weak shafts of light, stirred up as he fenced with his oldest friend, who
seemed to be wearing a patched pair of pants that he'd cast off after a growth
spurt at Eton. He spared his opponent nothing, and it took a bit for her to catch
a breath to answer.

"I rather think it's at the end of your sword, Sebastian. That sharp thing."

"I didn't say where, I said what, Freddie. Why would he buy this dump
when there's a reasonably good house at Roxbury Park?" He executed a perfect
flying parry. Freddie overcompensated, slipped and landed on her well-padded
bottom on the hard stone floor with a thump.

He was a cur to engage her, but she had insisted on sword-play to start the
day. An insistent Frederica Wells was, in his long-suffering experience,
impossible to ignore. He was more than a foot taller and several stones heavier,
a visitor to the finest *salle d'armes* in Great Britain and the continent, fit and
fresh from his lengthy Grand Tour after a lackluster year at university. His
father had sent him off with a private tutor in the hopes of civilizing him, but
Sebastian had become crafty ditching the old bird. In fact, for the last four

months Sebastian had been wholly on his own. Mr. Tetley had thrust a purse at him at the Acropolis in Athens and washed his hands of him, preferring the duke's wrath to one more day with his scapegrace son.

Freddie had been stuck at home as all girls were, no doubt singing and painting and doing other useless things. Her fencing skills had improved some from the last time they went at it, but poor Freddie looked like she'd had two too many lemon tarts thrice daily. He recalled they were her favorite. Even at eighteen, she had not lost her baby fat. Her freckled face was red from exertion, but she grinned up at him like a cheerful pixie as he pulled her to her feet.

She pushed a sweat-soaked brown braid behind her ear. "You know your father's love of all things medieval. How could he resist? Didn't he tell you all about it yesterday?"

"If he did, I was not paying attention. You know how he bores me." The pater had rambled on yesterday about some of the structure dating to the eleventh century, not that Sebastian cared. Gray rock was gray rock, and his mind had drifted to visions of boiling oil or molten lead being poured down through the machicolations on the old man. At twenty-one, he saw nothing but the duke's disinterest in anything contemporary, including himself. His father had preferred to spend his time with his secretary and their dusty tomes and broken relics rather than his only son. The men traveled all over Europe outrunning Boney himself in their quest for medieval miscellany.

"Well, the story of the Goddard Castle is not boring in the least," Freddie said, her eyes lighting.

Blast. It seemed she had been bitten by the history bug as well. *Goddard Castle* indeed. The Archibald family crest and motto was stamped on virtually every flat surface. The castle was originally home to the Earls of Archibald, and had been called Archibald Castle until his father had the hubris to rename it after himself. "I suppose you're going to give me a lecture now, aren't you, brat?"

"Your tutor gave a thorough report. I know you care nothing for history, so I won't waste my time trying to enlighten you if he couldn't," Freddie said, taking no trouble to mask her superiority. "But we are at war with the French, so even a blockhead like you might see the fascination in this tale. But, nevermind. I'm sure you have plans for the morning. Seducing housemaids and whatnot."

She stomped off in the direction of the armory to return her foil. He followed, amused by the sway of her round backside. His old breeches looked fairly good on her.

"I know you're dying to tell me," he called after her. "You never could keep your mouth shut for any length of time."

She turned like a clockwork gear, as he knew she would. "Go to the devil, Sebastian Goddard!"

"Already there, Freddie." He smiled at her, hoping she wouldn't decide to raise her weapon and run him through. He leaned against a leaded window, praying it would hold his weight.

Her blue-gray eyes narrowed. "You have not changed one bit."

"*Au contraire.* The past two years abroad have been very educational."

"I'll bet. Not that I would ever know. You never wrote."

"I'm sure I did a time or two." But most of the things he'd seen and done could not be divulged to a young lady in a letter. He supposed Freddie qualified as a young lady. From the way her chest heaved, it seemed she had grown breasts. "But you're right about the war. It was difficult to find accommodations where that Corsican upstart hadn't mucked with."

"Your father was worried."

Sebastian rather doubted that, but held his tongue. He really was too old to be rebelling and railing against the pater. He'd turn into a cliché if he wasn't careful.

"Yet here I am, not a hair on my head harmed." Sebastian fluffed some up. He was rather proud of his hair. It was dark, thick, and curly. Women loved to run their fingers through it, and he loved letting them.

"He's very glad you're home."

"This isn't home, Freddie, and never will be." Sebastian thought the castle, whatever it was called, was the gloomiest place he'd ever seen. Parts of Yorkshire were indeed beautiful, but no one could ever claim Goddard Castle was. It rose on its motte from a bare landscape like a set of blind giant's blocks. Even in its prime, Sebastian was sure it had been ugly. There was no sense of symmetry, and more than half the structure lay in ruins, even after over a year of his father's occupation.

Sebastian wiped his brow with the back of his sleeve and gazed out. He counted two twisted trees and three oozy black patches in the brutal sweep of land beyond the fallen curtain wall from this vantage point alone. Thank heavens his father had filled in the moat, or he'd be tempted to drown himself. He did not know how he was going to survive this visit with his father without resorting to drink, drugs or murder. Fortunately, he'd come prepared.

He sighed. "Go on. I know you're salivating to tell me about the castle. You're bristling like a terrier after a rat."

"Hello, rat," she said, suddenly sunny again. She slid to the floor opposite, propping the blade up against the stone wall, and crossed her ankles. No, she was not a young lady yet.

"I'll skip ahead through the centuries, although the Archibalds played a large role in the Pilgrimage of Grace in 1536."

Sebastian looked at her blankly. He was no pilgrim.

"You know, the uprising over Henry VIII dissolving the monasteries. No? No matter. Anyway, the Archibalds have always been a prominent Catholic family in this part of the world. Some say that's why the last Earl of Archibald sided with the French, but I think he was just in it for the money. He ran the largest spy ring in Britain!"

Sebastian perked up. Money was always of interest to him. There was never enough of it, especially when his father kept spending his on ruined castles.

"What did he do with his blood money? He obviously didn't use it to repair this place."

"No one knows. But for years, all sorts of traitors walked these halls making their evil plans," Freddie said with enthusiasm.

"And dodged the falling timbers," Sebastian replied. "Bloody dangerous work, spying for the Earl of Archibald."

Freddie laughed. "We've found no bodies. But people do say the castle is haunted."

"Utter rubbish. What became of the treasonous earl?"

"He was stripped of his title and lands for colluding with the French, and threw himself off the roof, plummeting to his death into the slimy water surrounding the keep to avoid the hangman's noose," she said with a dramatic flourish.

"Bloodthirsty wench." While Sebastian had been traveling, his father had paid the Crown what Sebastian considered to be a fortune for the property and renamed it. Who had been madder, old King George, the Earl of Archibald or Phillip Goddard, seventh duke of Roxbury? It was a near thing, one Sebastian was glad he wouldn't have to judge. He was not particularly impartial.

"So that's the recent history of Goddard Castle. And now your family has a chance to add to it."

"I won't be here long enough. As soon as this damned house party is over, I'm leaving." His father was in alt about refurbishing the castle, but as far as Sebastian was concerned, the place was still a death trap.

"Your father is tremendously excited, you know," Freddie said, interrupting his brooding. "He and my father have been closeted in the library for weeks making plans. There's to be a fancy dress ball tonight. What will you wear, Sebastian?"

"Evening clothes, I expect. Dressing in disguise is for children on All Hallows Eve."

Freddie's brows knit. "Spoilsport. I bet you a shilling you will not recognize me."

"I haven't a shilling to spare, brat. Travel is ruinously expensive, you know."

Freddie scrambled up and joined him at the window. The view did not seem to trouble her, but she must be used to it after living here for a while. "Was it very wonderful?"

Sebastian noted the wistfulness in her voice. He wasn't about to tell her all the 'wonderful' things he'd seen and done—her definition of wonderful would doubtless differ from his.

"It was all right. A pity I had to miss Paris and Parisian ladies, but I made do. You know I thought about enlisting so I could conquer France sooner."

Freddie nodded. "Uncle Phillip was quite upset when he received that letter. "

"So upset he dictated *his* letter to your father to write for him. I don't believe I'd even recognize His Grace's handwriting." Poor Wells must have had fits translating his father's rage to paper.

"An heir to a dukedom can't risk getting shot at."

"Whyever not? It's not as though the Dukes of Roxbury have ever amounted to much. I daresay the Archibalds on the wall over there are more useful, except for the last one."

"You have obligations. Responsibilities."

Sebastian snorted. "Like my father? If he turned up in the House of Lords, not a soul would recognize him. He hasn't been to Roxbury Park in ages. The place is going to rack and ruin. I stopped there before I came north." And discovered his father had bought himself a castle.

"Oh, dear. I didn't know."

He and Freddie had run wild at Roxbury Park, at least until his mother died. After that, he was mostly farmed out to relatives, or spent holidays at school with masters who were paid extra to watch him. He'd had a lonely childhood, but then so had Freddie. She had no mother at all to remember, and a father who jumped at the sound of his father's command and left her behind when he carried the duke's valises from one antiquarian auction to the next.

"So don't lecture me. You haven't the first idea of what's what in this world."

Freddie punched his arm with a chubby fist. "Next you will tell me I'm 'just' a girl. You are the same insufferable, conceited ass you always were."

"And you love me for it, brat." Sebastian stepped backward, expecting another blow, but Freddie was still as a stone, her fists clenched, her face crimson. "Steady. You know I'm only teasing you. Come, let's put our weapons away, swords and tongues both. I believe I have housemaids to corrupt, do I not? Do you have any recommendations amongst the staff?"

This time she aimed higher, but Sebastian pivoted and protected his jaw. "Have pity, Freddie. My face is my fortune. How am I to marry an heiress if you maim me? She'll have to be filthy rich to cover all my debts and the pater's besides."

"I feel sorry for the poor wretch already. You'll make a miserable husband."

"I agree, and have no intention of becoming one anytime soon. Good lord, you don't suppose the old boy's invited prospective brides here for me, do you? Perhaps I will have to wear a disguise after all. I can go as a hunchback. A leper."

Freddie walked across the gallery to pick up her foil. "I can tell them you're disgusting, if that will help keep them at bay."

"Capital! Mention all my vices. Make some up when you run out."

She looked at him with scorn, then set off down the hall. "I won't need to dissemble. You've given me plenty to work with."

"Freddie, Freddie. Such a shrew you are. And I thank you for it."

They entered the armory, a vast space newly filled with deadly and deteriorating weaponry. Standing on tiptoe, she tried unsuccessfully to return the sword to its bracket.

"Here, brat, I'll do it. I take it you've stopped growing."

"Only vertically. There seems to be no limit to the horizontal," she muttered.

"You'll find some man who likes you as you are. As long as you don't talk." And with that parting shot, he found it prudent to jog away from her and run through the warren of corridors and stairwells to his room. There was not a thing to do up here but wait for the masquerade party to commence tonight. Sebastian had met some of the guests over breakfast—not a soul was under fifty. A few more were arriving today, but no doubt they would be equally ancient. The duke had the clever idea of housing most of them in the dungeons. Sebastian really couldn't distinguish the dungeons' condition from the bedchambers—everything was primitive. Sebastian's own room was a spare as a monk's cell, although he had noted his father's to be filled with all the trappings of comfort. A massive gilt bed. Tapestries hanging on the walls. Carpets. And chairs whose upholstery was not fraying. Quite a difference from the rest of the dwelling.

But Sebastian would never spend a minute in the duke's room. Once the pater popped off, this castle and all its contents would be sold to the highest bidder.

Sebastian rummaged through his traveling trunk and found what he needed to pass the day. He filled his pipe with hashish, saving the opium for later, once the festivities began. His Grand Tour had been, as he told Freddie, very educational. He'd picked up a few bad habits and was glad of it. A mellowing of his senses came in handy when he had to encounter his father for any length of time.

Not that he often had. The duke was much too busy with other things. He was very good at ordering Sebastian about from a distance, but when confronted with him in person, tended to retreat into his library or abscond on a trip. He'd given Sebastian a quick tour of the castle yesterday, more to spout off knowledge than welcome his only son home after two years.

No matter. Sebastian would make his own fun. There might be a wayward wife to seduce, or Freddie to torment. The evenings ahead were likely to be dead bore, but he could endure it for a few days.

He took a deep draft of his pipe, felt the lassitude creep into his limbs. Yes, he could endure it. Especially knowing that in two days' time, he'd never see Goddard Castle again if he could help it.

5634862R0

Made in the USA
Charleston, SC
14 July 2010